He doesn't pet or pat or scratch me, just . . . hangs his arm over me. Like a buddy. An equal. I perk up.

We're teammates.

"No offense, buddy, but the way to survive middle school is to lay low. Stay under the radar. Be *invisible*. Having a huge German shepherd follow you everywhere is way *above* radar, you know? Geez."

Survive?

Well, now.

No one told me middle school was a matter of life or death.

And it's nice to know my dad and Madden agree: being *invisible* is the best kind of existence. Invisible is safe. That is all the confirmation I need.

I tighten my jaw, lift my chin. *You can count on me, Madden. I will not let you down. We will survive. We will remain invisible. You have my solemn vow.*

My mission here is clear: keep Madden from standing out in middle school.

ALSO BY **KRISTIN O'DONNELL TUBB**

A Dog Like Daisy

Luna Howls at the Moon

KRISTIN O'DONNELL TUBB

ZEUS
DOG OF CHAOS

 KATHERINE TEGEN BOOKS
An Imprint of HarperCollins Publishers

Katherine Tegen Books is an imprint of HarperCollins Publishers.

Library of Congress Cataloging-in-Publication Data

Names: Tubb, Kristin O'Donnell, author.
Title: Zeus, dog of chaos / Kristin O'Donnell Tubb.
Description: First edition. | New York, NY : Katherine Tegen Books,
 [2020] | Audience: Ages 8–12. | Audience: Grades 4–6. | Summary:
 "Zeus, a German shepherd, is assigned to Madden as a diabetic alert
 dog and must help him navigate middle school"—Provided by publisher.
Identifiers: LCCN 2019035470 | ISBN 978-0-06-288593-7 (hardcover) |
 ISBN 978-0-06-288594-4 (paperback)
Subjects: CYAC: Working dogs—Fiction. | German shepherd dog—
 Fiction. | Dogs—Fiction. | Diabetes—Fiction. | Middle schools—Fiction.
 | Schools—Fiction. | Single-parent families—Fiction.
Classification: LCC PZ7.T796 Zeu 2020 | DDC [Fic]—dc23
LC record available at https://lccn.loc.gov/2019035470

Typography by Andrea Vandergrift
21 22 23 24 25   PC/BRR   10 9 8 7 6 5 4 3 2 1
❖
First paperback edition, 2021

For the hikers: Alisha, Carla, Courtney,
Erica, MK, Lauren & Sarah
And for the young readers and their families who
manage diabetes daily

★ 1 ★

THE MOST DANGEROUS ASSIGNMENT OF THEM ALL

Valedictorian. That's a human word. It sounds important, far more important than the small human words that make it up:

Valid. Accurate or authentic.

Dick. Short for *detective*, a bloodhound. Like Sherlock Holmes.

Tory. Cautious, prefers the status quo.

An. Single. One.

So I figure a *valedictorian* is a single, accurate bloodhound who prefers the status quo, for things to stay *exactly* the way they are. That seems like a very specific label for these humans to give me, but they've given it to me nonetheless, so I'll try my hardest to live up to it.

1

Valedictorian. It's the most important word in the class. The word is so valuable, it makes my pointy ears pointier, my lush whiskers twitchier, my waggy tail waggier. I sit up even more straight, if that's possible. The silly hat the humans have balanced between my ears slides around on my head. It's flat and has a tassel hanging off one side. I have to tilt my head to keep it from falling off.

It must make me look bewildered, because Beef laughs at me. *Let me know if you're confused, Zeus,* he mutters from the corner of his big drooly mouth. *I'd be happy to explain it to our "valedictorian."*

I scowl. Beef knows we're not supposed to talk right now. Hooligan.

Beef is a Great Dane, and he takes that label *great* seriously. He towers over the rest of us at four feet tall, and he is a knot of muscle. You know the type: this fella's had a face full of whiskers since he was eleven months old. His bark is deep and sure. His collar is like a yoke, his neck is so thick. And his breath? Whew. Beef puts the *noxious* in *obnoxious.*

Dave McGruff, the head trainer, walks to the front of the room. I love Dave. So much so that my heart gets the best of my mouth and I shout out, *I love you, Dave!*

Beef and the other dogs laugh. *Teacher's pet,* they say.

I know that *teacher's pet* is a fancy human phrase

that means *favorite*, but I can't stand being called a pet. That isn't the role of a service dog. *I'm not a pet, I'm a tool*, I say.

Vader, on the opposite side of Beef, snorts a laugh through his smooshed Boxer nose. He manages to make it sound like a sneeze, though. *A tool!* he whines.

That you are, Zeus, Beef says with a nod. *That you are*.

Dave clears his throat into a microphone. Everyone quiets, because Dave is the alpha dog around here at Canine College. Dave has spiffied up his jumpsuit by adding a bow tie, and when I look closer, I see it's left over from the bow ties and bows they've put on us dogs today. I'm surprised the prison guards have let him do this, but then again, it *is* an important day.

"'The strength of the pack is the wolf, and the strength of the wolf is the pack.' Rudyard Kipling said that. I think it's the perfect description of our outstanding class of dogs here." Dave sweeps his hand in our direction. "Dogs not only make the world a better place, they make the world a safer place. They guard us. They protect us. They do whatever they can for their pack." Dave smiles, the human version of wagging. I want to wag back, but I'm in *sit*. And Dave knows that I love him, right? I get a little panicky, because what if he doesn't know? I haven't told him so since just a minute ago. But I do. I love Dave. I tell him as loudly as I can with my eyes: *I love you, Dave!*

"And dogs, see, they don't do all their hard work for glory, or for fame, or for a reward of any kind," Dave continues.

Not me, Beef mutters. *I'm definitely in it for the bacon treats.*

Vader snuffles a laugh.

"No reward," Dave continues, almost as if he heard our chatter. "No, dogs help us because of their perfect love. They are nothing but walking hearts, pure souls on four legs, these brave dogs before us today." Dave removes his glasses. I like it when humans remove their glasses. It makes it easier for me to label them with a word. Dave's word is *authentic*. Always has been.

"These dogs have all passed the Canine Good Citizen test and at least one other trial, usually a scent test, that determines their placement. They are all *good dogs*."

Good dog. That's the second-best label you can get. I can't help it: I wag.

Dave replaces his glasses, and his face tilts into a smile. "If you ask me, angels probably don't have wings. They have paws."

The humans have gathered in this room: the big, smelly cafeteria inside this big cage, a kennel that humans call a *prison*. This is where we've done most of our training since we were pups. Volunteers and the people who live inside this prison run Canine College. These humans are all here today, and they pound the palms of their hands together, which is called *applause* and as best as I can tell is like barking.

I have an itch under my vest, twitching my skin. But I can't scratch it. I'm in the vest, after all. That would be a violation. *Violation* is a fancy human word for *no*.

Dave looks down at the marks he's made on paper. "We work hard to place each dog in an assignment where we feel their gifts are best utilized. We take these assignments seriously, and we put hours of thought into each pairing. The last thing we want is for a human and his dog to be a mismatch. We strive for zero *re-assignments*."

At that word, every dog in the class stiffens. Our jaws collectively tighten. *Reassignment*. It's another fancy human word, one that is like wearing a forever Cone of Shame.

Reassignment definitely equals *failure*. And I can't fail. No one in my family has ever been reassigned, and I won't be the first.

Pssst. That'll be you, pal, Beef whispers to me, and Vader snuffles a laugh.

I blink. *What?*

I got twenty Milk-Bone dog biscuits that say you won't make it four weeks in your first assignment, Z. You will definitely be reassigned.

Vader is whimpering at this point, he's working so hard to hold in his laughter. I'm hotter than winter fur in July, but all I can manage to retort is, *YOU will be.*

Dave, up there at the podium, seems so certain of these assignments. I trust him and his authenticity. He looks at his stack of important papers and says, "So, without further ado, let's hear our pairings, shall we?"

Beef barks, *Yes!* and the audience laughs. Class clown.

"Vader Aloysius?" Huh. I didn't know Vader's middle name was Aloysius. Vader's handler leads him to the front of the cafeteria. "Vader here will be a bomb-sniffing dog for the NYPD!" Dave flips the tassel of Vader's hat to the other side, and the audience barks with applause. Vader's smirk says he's just as surprised to find himself graduating as we are.

"Melody Cookie?" Melody is assigned to a search-and-rescue team.

"Spark Pug?" Sparky will be an emotional support pug.

"Bo Addison?" Bo will work for the Coast Guard as a water rescue dog.

"Rosie Abeyta?" Rosie will be, as we all knew, a service dog to Colonel Victor Abeyta.

"Beeftastic Luckydog?" Beef winks at me, trots to the front of the room. "Beef here will work for an exclusive unit of New Jersey's K-9 division." Beef, wearing a badge? Well, I'll be flea-bitten.

"And now for our honored valedictorian." Dave smiles at me. My chin rises and my jowls pull back. *I love you, Dave!* "Our top dog has shown exemplary courage and intelligence. He is quick to pick up new commands, and he never, ever forgets his mission. This dog comes from a long line of heroes: both of his parents were K-9 dogs, and his grandfather was a search-and-rescue superstar."

I can hear my family drumming through my memories now: *Guten tag, Zeus. Chin up. Strong jaw. Tall ears.* And most loudly among these voices, my dad: *The best service dogs in the world are never seen. Just like your tail. You turn, your tail is gone. Be like your tail. Invisible is safe.*

Be your tail.

Be my tail. Be my tail. Be my tail.

Dave continues, "If ever there was a dog you can count on to do something by the book, it is this dog. Congratulations, Zeus Zagnut Zealousness!"

Beef and Vader double over with laughter at my full name. Here at Canine College, humans who donate a lot of money are allowed to name the puppies. Me, I got saddled with the old triple Z.

I walk to the front of the cafeteria, my heart pounding. My toenails click on the cold linoleum floor. Here it is: my life's calling! I've been training at Canine College for months so I, like the rest of my family, can be a hero. What will I be? A narcotics-sniffing dog? A K-9 commander? A cadaver recovery dog?

Dave stoops and looks me in the eyes: *authentic.* Words are labels, and they help you understand and categorize the world. My dad taught me to appreciate labels. *They're just like commands*, my dad used to say. *Commands are orders, and orders create order.*

Dave is earnest as he leans forward and whispers into my tall ear, "Zeus, you need this assignment as much as this assignment needs you." I'm not sure what he means by that. He flips my tassel and announces to the audience, "Zeus here will be a diabetic alert dog to a young man at nearby Page Middle School."

Middle school?

There is no barking applause.

There are no cheers or whistles or *attaboy, Zeus*es or words that feel like glorious fingernail scratches.

There might've been a gasp. Or two.

Based on the silence of the crowd (well, except for Beef, who snorfed a laugh), I realize:

Middle school must be the most dangerous assignment of them all!

★ 2 ★

THE BOY
WHO CAPTURES STARS

Assignment is good. *Reassignment* is bad. The bad
must all live inside the *re* part of the word, because:
A means singular. One.
Sign. Indication or warning.
Mint. Delicious zingy red-and-white candy.

When Dave and the other humans from Canine College discuss our *assignment*, I'm tail-wagging excited. I
love peppy mints, because minty-fresh drool is the best
kind of drool, and our *assignment* is what we've been
working toward this whole time. I await my candy.

But instead of candy I get a human. My new
human's name is Madden, and he comes to my school
at the prison later that same day. I've trained with him

in the past, but I didn't know he'd end up being my *assignment*. Canine College has a lot of volunteers who take us out of the prison during the sunny yellow hours for "real-world" training, which always confused me because isn't all of it the real world? Anyway, when I'd trained with Madden, I thought he was one of those volunteers. Temporary. *Temporary* is a fancy human word that means *just for now*.

Madden's a young pup, not much taller than the tips of my ears. He's on the small side; I'm on the tall side—we're a matched set. Today he has on a hat that is backward, so a big tuft of hair sticks out the front of it, like a forehead tail. He chews gum vigorously; it's like chewing powers his whole body. And he wears glasses that are so dirty, I can't see his eyes clearly through the muck.

This human does things that don't make sense.

But this is my new human—MY NEW HUMAN!— so I wiggle hello, lick and prance and preen and wag. *Hello, my new human!*

"Hi," the boy says around his mouthful of gum. "How are you, boy?" I look at him closely, try to figure out his word. None comes to me. Between their smell and their sound, I can usually label each human quickly. Labeling is wise because it reminds you how to handle each person. It creates *order*. But I can't peg

Madden yet. Madden is *not quite* what he seems to be.

And then he does something weird. He doesn't pet me or hug me or scratch me. He just . . . looks at me. Like *he's* trying to figure out *my* word.

I can tell him my word: *practical*. So I tell him that: *I'm practical. That's not my name, of course. My name is Zeus. And I'm practical.*

Dave's gaze bounces between the two of us like a tennis ball. "Madden's mom and I will be right outside filling out paperwork while you two practice commands, okay?"

I hadn't even noticed Madden's mom. That usually happens when someone doesn't notice *me* as well. Invisibility is mutually agreed upon.

Invisible is a good thing for a service dog. It is the goal.

Madden's mother and Dave leave. Madden and I look at each other longer. I inhale and realize what I should monitor for Madden: his honey-scented blood. His blood has chemicals in it, medicine. It smells almost like plastic. I know right away that I'm supposed to let him know if his blood changes. If it drops too salty, if it flutters too squeaky sweet.

Madden squats next to me. His chewing gum pops. He nods, but I don't know why; no one has asked a question. There is nothing to agree with.

"Listen, Zeus," Madden says quietly. "You . . . weren't my idea."

You weren't my idea, either, I say. I'm not sure what that means, but it sounded like I needed to say that right there.

"My mom really wanted me to get a dog for my diabetes, which is *so stupid*, because I have all this tech that does the same stuff. Two years, I've been doing it this way. I mean, I made it to eleven without you."

I made it to eleven without you, too. Now I'm really confused because I don't know what any of this means, but I learned in school that it's very important to mirror what your human does, and I don't want to mess any of this up. This isn't how I pictured getting paired with my new human.

I try to puzzle it out like I learned to do in school: all I know is that eleven is a human number. Numbers might as well be clouds, the way they shift and change shape and move out of view. You can't chew a cloud. I don't trust anything you can't chew.

Madden sits. His smell flushes sour, like garbage. Not dangerous, but sad.

At last, he hangs an arm across my neck. He doesn't pet or pat or scratch me, just . . . hangs his arm over me. Like a buddy. An equal. I perk up.

We're teammates.

"No offense, buddy, but the way to survive middle school is to lay low. Stay under the radar. Be *invisible*. Having a huge German shepherd follow you everywhere is way *above* radar, you know? Geez."

Survive?

Well, now.

No one told me middle school was a matter of life or death.

And it's nice to know my dad and Madden agree: being *invisible* is the best kind of existence. Invisible is safe. That is all the confirmation I need.

I tighten my jaw, lift my chin. *You can count on me, Madden. I will not let you down. We will survive. We will remain invisible. You have my solemn vow.*

My mission here is clear: keep Madden from standing out in middle school.

"Who wants to go for a ride?" Dave asks the question.

I bark.

We get in a big truck. I am in the back seat, and the windows are down, and I love *who wants to go for a ride?* so much. But Dave doesn't get in, too. *Dave doesn't get in, too!*

I knew this day was coming, of course. But here it is, surprising me like stinging, icy snowflakes.

I won't whine. I won't.

I whine. Dave blinks a couple of times.

I love you, Dave.

"I love you, Zeus. You're gonna be a superstar."

We drive away. Dave lives in the prison, so he can't come with us. Lots of us service dogs are trained in prisons by the people who live there, who never leave there. So now I have to leave Dave behind those bars.

My heart feels like the gravel crunching beneath these tires. Soon, outside rushes in through the window and hugs me with chilly wind, wind that smells like ice cubes and frosty leaves and pale sunshine. My fur tinkles. I feel better, because I have a *mission*!

Madden's mother drives. She smells like cleaning chemicals, crisp and blank as paper, and she moves like a ticking clock, *tickticktick*. Her word is obviously *precise*. Precise like clicking toenails. Precise like clippers snipping my fur. Yes, that's her word. It is easy to love someone who is precise. You know exactly what you are getting.

We pull up to a small shack with a man inside. Madden's mother hands over a tiny plastic card with her picture on it, and the fellow glances at it. "You guys get a pet, Lieutenant?" the man in the small shack says. He smiles at me.

Pet? I am no mere pet. This person obviously doesn't see my Vest of Importance. I shift so he can see my rank.

"Not exactly," Madden's mother says, at the same time Madden says, "Yes."

Yes? I harrumph. A *pet*! Madden is . . . maddening. Now I see where he gets his tag.

"Not exactly?" The man in the small house cocks his head and hands the plastic card back to her.

The lieutenant leans her elbow over the window. "I haven't had a dog in years, Jared. We'll see how this one works out. They're amazing, what they can do. I've seen it with my own two eyes. But I just like knowing I can pick up and go if I have to, you know?"

Jared smiles. "Military mind and a wandering heart."

The lieutenant nods curtly. "You know it." The man salutes, and the lieutenant salutes in return.

We drive down a road where all the houses look the same. Same, same, same. I don't rely on my sight much to guide me (eyes are the best liars, after all), but I hope our house smells different enough from these others so I can navigate around here. Right now, this is a muddle of sameness. It's like that time a volunteer took me into the Maze of Mirrors at the county fair while I was still training. I've never been so dizzy, seeing all those glass Zeuses! I remember whining a lot.

I should maybe whine now.

But I shouldn't have worried. We turn into a driveway, and our house smells crisp and sharp, like bleach.

So harsh it burns my nostrils a bit, and I sneeze.

"This is it, Zeus," Madden says, tapping his leg. I am proud of him, knowing right away how to communicate the command *come* with hand signals. Even though he thinks I'm a pet. I'll train him. "Come on."

I leap from the truck and land—*brrrr!*—on a patch of ice, cold and slickery. I skid, slide, and fall into a prickle bush.

Madden chuckles but asks, "You okay, bud?"

I huff. My breath comes out in an icy puff.

"Let's go upstairs."

I follow Madden into the house. I haven't been in a lot of houses, because I've been mainly living in a prison with Dave, but this one feels more like my veterinarian's office than a place to live. There are no soft cushes on the floor, no colorful things on the wall. The furniture is small and hard and plastic and reminds me of pebbles stuck to my paw. The house is hollow, and it echoes. Echoes make a heart feel lonely.

We trot up the stairs, my toenails *click-click-click-ing* on the cold, wood floors. When we enter Madden's room, my heart gasps. He has a huge thing hanging from the middle of his ceiling, with nine floating multicolored spheres bobbing gently in wide circles, all orbiting a big yellow ball. It reminds me of dogs circling, testing out new relationships by not getting too

17

close, but not ceding any power by backing too far away. It feels . . . *familiar*, but I can't label it. And I can't really explain it, but looking at it makes me feel small.

And somehow—somehow!—Madden has brought stars *inside*. They cover his ceiling, twinkling and blinking. They glow greener in here than they do outside, but this boy has captured *stars*. I believe I've underestimated him.

Madden plops into a big poof, and it crinkles like a wad of paper. He reaches under his bed, pulls out a box, and swings the lid open. The can he produces opens with a *whoosh*, and the bubbles fizzing and hissing against the tin can sound like mini firecrackers.

Should I smell smoke?

Madden squints at me. I squint back. "Have you ever had a soda, Zeus?"

I haven't, but this feels like a challenge somehow, so I respond, *Have you ever had mouse guts, Madden?*

And then something wild happens. Humans don't hear dogs; every dog knows that. Infuriating but true, because we are rather brilliant and pithy, and it would make my job oh so much easier if humans could just hear me with those tiny, ineffective ears of theirs. But Madden laughed just then, when I said that, and for a moment—a sliver of a moment—it was like we had *talked*.

Madden pushes himself out of his chair and grabs a paper cup from his bathroom. He returns and pours brown, firecrackery liquid into it. "Here," he says, placing the fizzy cup in front of me. "Drink up."

I sniff it, and bubbles shoot up my nostrils like tiny buzzing gnats. I sneeze. I paw my nose. I rub my face on the carpet. Madden laughs. I squint at him again.

I slurp the liquid. And oh—*oh!* It is sweet and syrupy and fizzy and it feels like bumblebees dancing on my tongue, light and airy and bubbly and unpredictable and I sneeze sneeze sneeze and I slurp the whole thing up and then chew on the waxy cup. *Oh!*

I can see how this boy captures stars.

Madden laughs until tears pop out of his eyes. His heart gallops strong and happy. We are joyful and drinking bubbles and capturing stars! Until . . .

Madden's door swings open.

"Madden Phillip Malone. What in heaven's name do you think you're doing?"

The lieutenant stands in the doorway, fists hammered on hips. "Zeus can't drink soda! And you! Are you kidding? You know what this does to your blood sugar!"

This is the smoke I was supposed to smell earlier.

"It's diet soda, Mom," Madden mutters.

The lieutenant sweeps through the room, gathering

up my yummy chewy star-filled bubble cup and Madden's can of firecrackers. She lifts the edge of the blanket on his bed and finds his box, checks its contents.

Her questions pop at him like a yanked leash: "When was the last time you checked your blood sugar? Where's your test kit? Did you check your CGM? What did it say? Did you bolus? How much insulin did you take?"

Madden mumbles and stumbles across his answers like he's treading through thick mud, his voice swampy.

"Speak up, son," the lieutenant says. She huffs. "Mad, it's cold out, and you know how much harder your body has to work when it's cold, right?" Then the lieutenant does this odd thing: she chews on her fingernails. Her *fingernails*, the absolute best part of a human! This is very odd grooming indeed.

The air hangs heavy; the orbs overhead sway. Madden's mom shakes her head.

"No more people food for Zeus," the lieutenant says. "He cost too much money to get sick on us. And no more soda, Madden." She slams his bedroom door—*bam!*—and stomps away.

"It's *diet* soda!" Madden yells after her. He sighs, and I feel all the weight of the wind behind it. He lifts his chin toward the door. "Let me tell you something, Zeus. My mom? In and out of the country for the last ten years. Deployed all the time. She loves her job more than anything." He stops there for some reason, letting that phrase, *more than anything*, snap like a too-short leash.

"I've lived with my grandparents since I was like three years old . . . ," he continues. He looks at a photo on his desk, of two people in hiking gear standing on top of a mountain. As he does, his heart, which had the scent of a smoky red coal, cools to simmering orange. "They're my dad's parents, not hers," he adds, "so it gets weird."

I hear what he's *not* saying. Humans do that a lot: *not* say the things that are actually the most important things. And what Madden *not*-says is this: *My grandparents and my mom don't belong to each other. They aren't a pack.*

"Yeah, I lived with them until she got reassigned. Here. The army gave her a crummy desk job."

WHOA WHOA WHOA.

Back up.

The lieutenant, *reassigned*?

Reassigned is the worst of all the words. Every dog knows that.

I blink at the door she just slammed. Huh. *Precise* isn't her label after all. It's *reassigned*. Because once you are given that label, it follows you around forever. My forehead crinkles. This is a worrisome new development.

"She's got to hate it, her new job. She loves traveling and being gone." That last word, *gone*, is as hollow as this house. "Her guilt got the best of her, I guess, so she made me move here, too. She hovers over me, when I've been managing by myself since my diagnosis two years ago. Nana and PopPop trusted me to handle things myself, but my mom? Total helicopter. And now she made me get you. I mean, a *service dog*? Really?"

Madden reaches over and scratches under my chin. He's not supposed to do that while I'm wearing my vest. When I'm wearing my vest, I'm working. But, *oh*, chin scratches feel like sparks of love. *Fingernails.* I lift my chin higher. I feel guilty as stolen dog treats for enjoying this in my vest, but c'mon! *Fingernails!*

"If you were really a *pet*, I mean, yay! A dog!" Okay, that is a good sign. He knows my true role as a dog of service. "But I don't *need* you, Zeus. I don't need anyone." At this, he looks at the picture of the hikers again, and his scent changes to a subtle sour smell, like spoiled milk. His words ring of untruth. He needs *them*.

The colorful orbs float silently above, in the midst of all those green glowy stars. There's me at the center, and the circles drawn around me, the new humans who are keeping me barely within their orbit: the lieutenant,

22

who isn't sure about me because she has a runaway heart and I'm a *stay!* kind of creature, and Madden, who doesn't like me because I am the opposite of his independence.

This mission is going to be rawhide tough.

★ 3 ★

WELCOME TO BAND

Middle school puts the *P-U* in *puberty*. My nose happens to be exactly halfway between tail end and armpit on each one of these kids. It's the "high-sniff" zone. And there are so many hormones it makes my stomach churn like I've eaten too much grass. Hormones smell like a newly tarred road on a hot summer day: growth but not yet *grown*.

The hallways are wide and cold, and the floors are so shiny slick I have to tread lightly, like I'm slipping over an icy puddle. This building looks a lot like Dave's prison, but with boxes instead of bars.

Hundreds of metal boxes line the halls. Madden keeps his eyes lowered, a submissive stance in dog

24

language. I mirror it as much as I can, but kids keep swooping in front of me, causing me to skid into them.

Madden's skin is warm but painful, like a sunburn. Embarrassment. Why does his confidence smell as gritty and dry as cat litter?

"Dude, you get to bring your dog to school?"

"Lucky!"

"Can I pet him?"

Madden is supposed to say no, of course. I'm a service animal. I am *wearing my vest*. I am supposed to receive no attention while on the job. But Madden = maddening. So he says, "Yeah, sure. He loves chin scratches."

But I don't—

Zing zap zam!

Oh. *Yeah*. Chin scratches!

It feels so guilty good, my back leg thumps against the cold slick floor—*thumpthumpthump*. The kids laugh like shiny jewel-toned June bugs and I have to remind myself how undignified this is, but *chin scratches*.

We finally manage to weave and slip through the crowd, and I can hear the windy whispers all around us:

"He has diabetes."

"Does he have seizures?"

"Nope, wrong sickness, stupid."

"You can have seizures with diabetes."

"I want to bring my dog to school. No fair."

"Yeah, well, he has to stick himself with needles all the time. You want to be a pincushion like him? Then you can bring your dog, too."

"Ew, no. Needles are the worst."

"I know, right?"

More kids pack the hallway, and it's so tight and stuffy and hot and loud and hormoney. My head spins. The students bang open and close the metal doors—I hear someone call it a *locker*—and the clatter reminds me of the time that a training volunteer took me to the bank to drop off coins collected at a Canine College fund-raiser. The lady at the bank poured the coins into this huge machine, and *clank-clang-clunk*, the coins got sorted.

Middle school hallways feel like living inside that *clank-clang-clunk* machine.

Suddenly, a feather of a girl floats in front of us. She has an ice-cream cone on her shirt and she has a long rainbow winding around her neck and she is shiny and golden in every way except she wears cat ears on her headband. If I squint, I can pretend they're dog ears.

"Hi, Madden!" she sings. She *sings*. Her voice is like a bluebird's, and it makes my tail wag, and I can't believe how quickly I've become so undignified. I snap to attention.

Madden's heart picks up a skippier beat, and the heat rising off his skin changes from sunburn red to soft and glowy, like skin warmed beside a fire. "Hi, Ashvi."

"Is this a service dog?"

"Yes."

Well, muzzle me. Madden tells the truth sometimes.

Ashvi stoops to look at me. Her eyes are like bronze pennies, and I love her so much it makes my toe pads tingle. But here's the thing: she doesn't pet me. She respects my duty. "What's your name, bud?"

Zeus. I love you.

"This is Zeus."

Ashvi smiles, and beams of sunlight bounce around her. "Zeus. The God of Chaos."

Chaos? Chaos is the opposite of order. *Chaos* isn't my label.

But Madden chuckles like that's the funniest thing he's ever heard. His laugh is too plastic. He should be more subtle. He should just tell her he loves her.

Ashvi stands and smiles at Madden, and Madden's insides melt all over the floor. I know I'm the only one who notices, though, because Ashvi walks right through Madden's entrails and places her hand on his arm.

"My granddad had a service dog. I don't know what you need him for, but Zeus is going to be a huge help."

27

She's perfect in every way. That's her word: *perfect*. Ashvi floats down the hall, slinging her rainbow wrap over her shoulder, trailing comets in her wake.

Madden sighs and slips into a trance. A happy trance like the smell of sizzling bacon grease, not a dangerous one that requires an alert from me. Definitely not subtle.

Then, a terrible, horrible screeching sound blasts through the air, so awful it makes the hair on my back hackle. I growl, get into fight stance. The sound is low, grinding, and it surely signals the end of the world. The pupils bounce off the walls and each other, swarming into rooms. Lockers clang like coins one last time, and Madden wakes up from his fuzziness and snaps tight like a rubber band.

"Crap, that's the late bell. C'mon, Z!"

I escort Madden to a series of classes:

Science. Or as I think it should be called, the Study of Stuff. Madden and I weave through a maze of desks to get to his seat. I step gingerly over a lot of things and I bump into many of them, and the students laugh. Madden burns like the smell of scorched popcorn.

Math. Number Pushing. Madden and I enter the room, and a wall of squeals and whispers washes over us. Madden shifts in his skin like he has fleas.

NOISE BREAK! In prison, cafeterias were for food. In middle school, it is where noise is made, plus a bit of smelly chow. After he eats, Madden discreetly presses a button on a black plastic device attached to his belly, and the sweetness of his blood disappears behind chemicals. I hide under a long, squeaky table the whole time, because many kids point at me when I enter, and this makes Madden clench his face like a fist.

Next, Madden brings me *out*, to a courtyard surrounded on three sides by the school. He removes my vest and commands me to relieve myself. It is difficult, going to the bathroom with so few moments between those horrible "bells." Not to mention this whole courtyard has a fine, misty cloud hanging over it that reeks of scents that can only be called, I now know, *middle school*. Then the classes continue:

Social Studies. Dead People Who Did Things. Many pupils reach out their fingers to pet me as I pass, and I get all jittery and distracted. Based on the scowl Madden wears, he feels the same.

Next, Madden goes into a restroom. He looks at the machine attached to his arm, then he—*snap!*—staples the side of his finger, and the sound echoes around the room. Another kid pushes out of a stall and scowls at the sight of Madden's blood, smirks at the sight of me. Madden wipes a drop of blood on a piece of paper, then swipes his finger on his jeans. He compares the two screens and nods. "Blood sugar good," he whispers to me. I'm confused. *I know*, I say. *I would've told you if it was off.* A bell screams, and Madden and I obey and run.

Oh, *now* I get it! Bells are a *command*! That makes their terrifying shrieks slightly more tolerable.

Next, Language Arts, or the Glorious Study of Labels. Everything in this class is labeled, even the labels themselves! Labels have labels like *noun*, *verb*, *adjective*. I'm going to learn quite a bit in this class. I'm going to learn how to label people better! I *sneeze-sneezesneeze* with joy when I realize how much fun all this labeling is going to be. The other kids laugh. Madden goes boneless and slumps into his seat.

Today in the Glorious Study of Labels, the students read a poem:

so much depends
upon

a red wheel
barrow

glazed with rain
water

beside the white
chickens

Do I understand this poem? No. Does it make my teeth itch, wanting to *barkbarkbark* and chase those darned white chickens all over the farmyard? Yes.

And then, after an unending number of those horrid shrieking commands called *bells*, we walk to a room at the end of a long hall. Madden ditches his too-heavy backpack on a shelf, and before we even walk through the door, his face brightens, his steps become springier, his heart peps. He swings open the double-wide door and whispers down to me, "Zeus, welcome to Band."

★ 4 ★

MUSIC MUST BE DESTROYED

*I*nstrument:

    In. To be contained; the opposite of *out.* (I prefer *out.*)

    Strew. To cover or scatter.

    Mint. Red, zippy round candies.

    As best I can tell, an *instrument* scatters musical notes and *not* candy, as its label implies. Why am I never given the candy I am promised? When we walk inside the band room, the air is filled with a confetti cloud of notes, flitting and honking and pounding and plinking all about. A confusing whirlwind of sound. I blink. I pant.

Madden goes to a locker at the back of the room—*bam!* Must lockers always be slammed?—and pulls out a huge, black suitcase. "C'mon, Z."

We then move toward Madden's chair, but the band room is *crowded*, littered with cases (which I sniff: no candy. Just . . . human drool?), chairs, and these tall sticks with top hats that Madden calls *music stands*.

Madden's chair is one chair in from the right side of the room, and he and I try to *squeeeeeeeeze* in, but it is too tight and I spin and I pant and I spin and at last I sit and a small metal thing jabs me in the rear end, and I LEAP up with a squeal.

"Ewwwwww," the girl to the left of Madden says. "That dog sat on my mouthpiece!"

The rest of the class laughs, and I wish for *them* to all go sit on a mouthpiece, thank you very much.

I get up and spin again. I knock over a music stand. Some of the students around me huff and roll their eyes. Madden's skin reddens like a sunburn again, but I must sit next to him. I know my duty.

The student to the right of Madden shoots his hand in the air. "Mrs. Shadrick?" he shouts. "Um, we need to discuss this *dog situation*."

The tone of his voice makes me hang my head, tuck my tail. I'm just trying to do my job.

Mrs. Shadrick looks over the edge of her glasses from the front of the room. "Oh! There's a dog!"

The students laugh again, and all eyes turn to me. Madden could power a small city with the heat coming off his skin. This is WAY ABOVE RADAR, as Madden would say.

Mrs. Shadrick's eyes dart between me and Madden and Mr. Dog Situation. "Jake, switch chairs with Madden."

The room gasps. It feels like a tiny tornado. I'm surprised the pieces of paper on the music stands aren't swept up into it.

I had no idea chairs were so meaningful.

Mr. Dog Situation, whose name is apparently Jake, glares red laser eyes at me, at Madden, then turns them on Mrs. Shadrick. "But Madden didn't *earn* this seat! This is first chair!"

Madden shifts on his tailbone. "Mrs. Shadrick, it's okay. I—"

Mrs. Shadrick whips off her glasses and glares at Jake. She is *not* afraid of red laser eyes, and I like her because of this superpower. Her word is *business*.

"Jake," she says. "Switch chairs with Madden."

Jake stands. He kicks his instrument case toward the seat where Madden now sits. It slides across the dirty linoleum and hits me in the ribs. Madden's eyes snap off the floor. He stands, too. He is a head shorter than Jake, but he locks eyes with him. It's what dogs do when they're ready to battle.

"Don't kick your case at my dog, dude," Madden says. "Don't *ever* do anything that will hurt Zeus."

This sudden display of pack loyalty from Madden surprises me. Loyalty is splendid, like a clean, new collar: always there, supporting you, tags announcing with a jangle whose pack is yours. I still don't have a word for him yet. No label. *Surprising*, maybe?

As we squeeze by Jake into what is apparently the first chair, Ashvi floats into the room on a ray of sunshine. My tongue lolls. I wag.

Ashvi sits several rows ahead of us but turns and winks at me. "Hi, Zeus! Hi, Madden!"

"Hi, Ashvi!" Madden and I sing in unison back. We are decidedly Not Subtle.

Mrs. Shadrick taps a long stick on her music stand, and I sit at attention, because *Stick!* Surely she is going to throw it at any moment. I will show these students who *rules* at Stick!

(Me. It's me. I rule at Stick.)

"Noah, will you write the counting in for 'The Imperial March' on the whiteboard, please?"

A kid walks to the front of the room, a small piece of wood bobbing between his lips. He apparently likes Stick, too.

"*Without* your reed, Noah. You can make out with your sax in a bit." This sends the room into gales of laughter, even Noah, who returns to his seat and spits the slice of wood into an open suitcase. These kids love their teacher. They love her *business*.

Squeak squeak, says the black marker on the whiteboard. Noah draws a series of blackbirds sitting on telephone wires:

"Excellent! All right, everyone, instruments up!"

The kids raise their instruments, some shiny and tangled and brassy, some twee and skinny and wooden, some sticklike with a puff of cotton on the end. Many kids play the same type of instrument; there are four kids who lift up the same shape of instrument as Madden's. Madden winces when he raises his large cone—his *tuba*, he called it. And I can see why he cringes: the brass part that rests against his body dings the black box attached to his skin, the one that gives him medicine. Madden heaves it higher, and his heart kicks up the pace.

Mrs. Shadrick flips a switch on a thing, and it ticks off time loudly and horribly, *TICKTICKTICKTICK*. Toes around the room begin to tap in the same rhythm.

"One, two, onetwothreefour!"

And then. And *then*!

The shiny, twisted, brassy, wooden, twee, skinny, puffy instruments all begin playing. At once. Together. It is a wall of sound. It is powerful and mighty, this pack all howling together.

The hair on my neck rises. My eyes water.

This! This is *music*!

And I know this music. It's from one of Dave's favorite movies, about stars and space and good and evil. They are making music! Here! Now!

Madden's cheeks puff and his lungs heave and his heart gallops. I smell the change in his blood all this exertion causes. It's not dangerous—not yet. But it's falling as fast as a raindrop from a storm cloud. This *tuba* obviously takes a lot of effort. How can something that takes this much effort make him happy?

"Very good!" Mrs. Shadrick shouts as she nods

along with the melody. "It builds here—keep it going!"

The music turns, and the sound gets wilder, louder.

"Let me FEEL the spit coming out of those trombones, guys!" Mrs. Shadrick shouts to a group of kids whose instruments slide back and forth.

I prick my ears, try to pick out a single instrument like Mrs. Shadrick apparently can. It's like trying to pick out a single puff of smoke from a plume.

And it scares me, honestly—these emotions, this sound. I realize why: I can't label it. There aren't good enough words to describe the sound of music.

How can I understand something if I can't label it? It's like trying to label Madden. Music and Madden are the same. Maddening.

Underneath the music I hear Madden's heartbeat: It is joyful. Clear. True.

Underneath the music I hear the instrument Mrs. Shadrick called a *flute*, Ashvi's flute, a bluebird like her voice.

"Are you a baseball player, Eli? Because you're swinging that mallet like a bat!" Eli, one of the drummers, swings more gently, and the drum mellows and blends more subtly.

Drums *boom* and trumpets *blare* and flutes *twee*, and then Mrs. Shadrick shouts, "Madden, take the tuba lead on this part!"

Madden shuffles, struggling under the weight of his instrument. The sound it makes is low, sad—like the sound of his heart when he looked at the photo of the hikers last night. But then his heartbeat blends with the music. Becomes the music. He smiles behind his mouthpiece, and his tuba smiles with him. He is all smiles and music and heartbeat at the moment. But his blood frowns, his sugar dropping with all this exertion.

Jake frowns, too, his scowl masked by his mouthpiece. But I can smell his discontent—it is slick and wobbly like undercooked bacon. Jake leans too far right, and his elbow bumps Madden's. Madden's tuba hiccups. I suspect Jake's word is *villain*.

Madden's part winds down, and the music swells, then silences. The last note of the song hangs in the air, humming like a nearby lightning strike.

My heart feels suddenly empty without the *booms* and *blares* and *twees*.

"Pretty good." Mrs. Shadrick nods, and she turns off the terrible *TICKTICKTICK* that had disappeared under the cozy blanket of music. "And Madden. You're really living up to that first chair. Outstanding."

Madden blushes as hot as a metal bowl full of water in the summer sun. Jake, beside him, turns on his laser eyes again. Ashvi smiles.

Outstanding?

OUTSTANDING?

Out: The opposite of *in.* Great stuff.

Standing: The opposite of *sitting.* Also great stuff.

Outstanding = great stuff. The opposite of *invisible.*

We are supposed to stay under the radar, *invisible,* in middle school. If my dad was clear on anything, it was this: *Stay as invisible as your tail, Zeus.* And yet here Madden is, being *outstanding.*

This will never do.

Music did this.

It is plain to see what I must do to keep my mission alive, to keep us invisible:

Music must be destroyed.

★ 5 ★

EAT THE BIRDS

I have my mission. My *duty*:

Do. To take action.

Tee. A precise fit, as in "to a tee."

I must take precise action to destroy music. But how?

"Tomorrow I'll hand out more sheet music for the holiday concert," Mrs. Shadrick says. She waves pieces of paper in her hand, *flipflipflip*, and they, too, are marked with blackbirds perched on telephone wires. "Be sure and add this to your notebook."

Then the air crackles.

"MRS. SHADRICK?" a voice from nowhere says. It is loud and comes from overhead—*Is this the Big Dog in the Sky?!* Except the Big Dog sounds more nasally than I would've expected. And angry. And crackly. And human.

Mrs. Shadrick turns to a box on her wall, looks up at it. "Yes?" MRS. SHADRICK CAN HEAR THE BIG DOG, TOO.

"MADDEN MALONE IS IN THERE, YES?" This voice—it *has* to be the Big Dog. The alpha. She knows exactly where Madden is. Madden warms next to me at the mention of his name, spoken from above.

"Yes."

The air sizzles. "HE NEEDS TO RIDE THE BUS HOME TODAY." And then the air crackles silent, taking the Big Dog with it.

Mrs. Shadrick peers over her glasses at Madden. "Got that?"

Madden nods, heat waves rising off his skin. "Yeah."

The demon bell screeches, and kids stumble and shuffle to put their instruments back in their cases, back in their lockers. *Blam! Squeak! Click click click!*

Madden waits, though, until most of them are gone. His eyes slide between me and the huge black case that holds his tuba. His sigh frowns.

I know what those slidy eyes, those frowny sighs mean: he's sizing up the situation. Madden can't handle both his tuba and me on this bus. We're both bulk.

My eyes get slidy, too, and I stare down the tuba case. *It's you or me, tuba.*

The tuba makes music with Madden's smile and heart.

And me? So far, I haven't even needed to alert Madden about his sugary blood. It's swayed and swooned a bit, particularly when he played his tuba, but it hasn't yet been dangerous.

Madden can't manage us both.

Will he choose me?

HE CHOSE ME!

I look at that smug, shiny tuba one last time. *Take THAT, tuba!* The tuba isn't petty, though; it remains silent. I whip my tail at it.

The bus chugs in the parking lot, spewing black smoke from its tail end like a dragon with gas. The doors swing open—*screeeee!*—and I can't help it: I pull backward a bit because of the green cloud of smell that wafts from inside. Salami and feet and body and soggy rubber.

Madden pops my leash. "C'mon, Z!" he hisses through clenched teeth, his eyes flicking to the line of kids behind us, waiting to get on the bus.

The steps are steep and slick. Madden and I climb them, and when I round the corner at the top of the stairs, the whole bus wails, "Awwwwwww!" It is a collective human exhale, full of heartbeats and smiling eyes. I lift my chin; I am aware that this human sound is made only around canines like me.

"Wait, is that your dog, dude?"

"He's so cuuuuuute!"

"What's his name?"

"*Maaaaaad*-deeeeeen! Did hims bring his pubby dog to school 'cause hims was lonely?"

"Jake, shut up."

Madden ignores them, and he smiles oddly, like a plastic doll. Plastic blood, plastic smile. His label surely isn't *plastic*, is it?

I follow Madden down the narrow aisle. He slumps into a squishy-hard green bench, and I curl up under his feet, beneath the seat in front of him. There's something black and sticky on the floor that pulls at my fur, and if they blame me for that puddle over there I will be upset.

The bus doors *heesh* closed, and the machine leaps forward with a growl. It is hot in here, steamy, like I imagine an overly full belly, and it bakes all the smells together—body and feet and sweat—into one huge middle schooler pie. I pant, because breathing through my nose is out of the question right now. I pant harder.

Riding a bus is *nothing* like the *whowantstogo-foraride* experience of a car. *Whowantstogoforaride* is open and wild and ripe with eating wind and bugs. Riding the bus is sticky and cramped, and I wouldn't want to eat ANYthing in here.

Madden leans his head against the cool glass and zones out. The bus starts and stops and starts and stops, and I think about my mission to destroy music and how exactly I can do that. A piece of paper folded into a triangle sails through the air—*whoosh!*—and skids to a halt under a seat three benches away.

Paper!

Music somehow came from all those birds sitting on wires, all those marks printed on the sheets of paper Mrs. Shadrick held. If I destroy the paper, if I *eat those birds*, the students can't play the songs.

I smile. My tongue lolls out of the side of my mouth. I can practically taste the task now:

Eat the birds.

★ 6 ★

ANGER SMELLS LIKE BUFFALO CHICKEN WINGS

When we get to Madden's house, the scene in the driveway terrifies me: the mouth of a truck is wide open, and the lieutenant is bent inside it, hanging over its metal teeth. I can only see her legs, her toes barely touching the ground. The truck is gobbling the lieutenant from the waist up! The truck clangs and clatters while chewing her. I stop short, feel the hackles of my fur stand along my spine. I low-growl.

Madden seems unfazed that this truck is eating his mother alive.

The lieutenant straightens. She has the car's digestive juices on her face, and she swipes them, leaving a black smear across her cheek. "Sorry I couldn't grab you from school. Stupid truck broke down again."

Madden pauses like he wants to say something, and I can practically taste his words hanging in the air like a hovering treat: *It's okay.* But he doesn't say it. I guess he doesn't really feel like it is okay.

The lieutenant lifts her chin at a metal box splayed open on the driveway. "Hand me a socket wrench?"

Madden and I cross to the metal box. Inside are rows of shiny metal things, things that look a bit like band instruments and their buttons. Tools. Madden pauses again.

The lieutenant smiles with half her face. "If I said hand me a bass sax, you'd know it."

Madden smiles with the other half of *his* face. If they'd put their faces together, they'd have a whole smile. "Well, yeah. They're kinda hard to miss. It is one *huge* saxophone. Best for—"

"How did Zeus do today?" The lieutenant lifts her chin at me next, just like she did at the tools in this box. *She* knows I'm a tool.

A whiff of anger—a fiery scent, a blend of sweat and heat like the smell of buffalo chicken wings—rises in Madden at being interrupted. "Fine, I guess. He didn't do anything except get in the way. Are we sure he knows what he's supposed to be doing for me?"

The lieutenant's jaw tightens. "I've seen what dogs

47

can do on the job, Madden." Her scent, which is usually as neutral as paper, is suddenly as salty as the ocean. "I've seen dogs like Zeus save lives. I once saw a German shepherd like Z sniff out a C-4 explosive in a parked car in the middle of Ghazni. That dog probably saved a dozen lives that day." She pauses there, and her scent is now a confusing mix of emotions: pain and happiness, like running too fast and suddenly finding yourself too far from home.

It's hard to believe her label is *reassigned*.

"Dogs are better than tech because things with a heartbeat want to keep hearts beating." She shrugs, turns back to the truck, and resumes banging it with her wrench.

"*Most* things with a heartbeat," Madden mutters. He studies the tips of his sneakers, which I understand, because they smell very interesting.

"What's that?" the lieutenant says, straightening.

"I have a CGM," he says, not repeating himself. "It does the same thing."

The lieutenant stoops next to me, and I can tell that while she is good at staring people down, she is less good at hugging people with her eyes. She scratches my neck, or, well, tries to. Her odd grooming habit of gnawing on her fingernails makes her ineffective in the scratching department.

"This dog can detect a drop in your blood sugar twenty minutes faster than that glucose monitor can," she says. "Give me a heartbeat any day over that tech of yours."

The way she says it—*that tech of yours*—makes the scent of buffalo chicken wings rise in Madden again. She's odd, the lieutenant. She said herself that she was unsure about having a dog, that having a dog meant she was pinned to one place. Why is she arguing *for* me now? And why is she calling me "a heartbeat"? Perhaps these confusing things contributed to her being *reassigned*.

"I'm going to get a snack," Madden says, turning on the toe of his interesting-smelling sneaker.

"What kind?" the lieutenant asks, straightening. "When did you last test? Low carb, okay? And remember to bolus. You've got to stay ahead of your blood sugar with your meds."

Now it is Madden's turn to low-growl. I know that should put me on guard, my human grumbling like that, but it makes me grin instead, watching this young pup stand up to the pack leader. "I got it, Mom. Geez!"

The lieutenant half sighs, half grumbles. "Don't do that, Mad. I get to worry. I believe I've earned the right to worry." I'm confused by that, because *earn* means *get treats*. Why would anyone want to earn worry?

She continues, "Oh, and I'd like to talk about the upcoming JDRF walk, Madden. I want to get a team together."

"Mom, no!" Madden's mood shifts from anger to stubbornness, a scent like two-day-old fish. "A fund-raising walk for diabetes? Don't do that. *Gah.*"

The lieutenant is unblinking. "Diabetes is part of who you are, Madden. Who *we* are. That won't ever change. I want to support the organization that helps fight it."

She bends back into the mouth of the truck and *clang bang clangs* her tools against the teeth of the machine.

Madden tugs my limp leash and mumbles so low I know the lieutenant and her tiny, ineffective human ears can't hear him: "Diabetes is the worst part of who I am."

My heart droops, bringing my ears and tail with it. Madden doesn't have worst parts, only different parts. *There is no* worst *in you*, I say, but of course he can't hear me.

All this sadness feels like cold wind, wind that whisks away and erases all the glorious scents.

★ 7 ★

JOY THROUGH
NOSTRIL EXPLOSIONS

Who wants to go for a walk?" Madden asks later, after this boring part of the day called *homework*, and I feel like every strand of fur on my body explodes into an exclamation point!

ME I WANT TO GO I DO ME PICK ME I AM SO SO GOOD AT WALK!

I bark. I spin in circles. I wag. I wag so big my tail knocks a potted plant off a table, and earthy black soil flies everywhere. I scowl at my tail, but tails don't listen. Tails don't have ears. You can't change a tail.

Tails are invisible—*humph*. Tell that to my hind end.

Madden huffs and fetches the growling tornado machine humans call the *vacuum*. He vacuums the soil off the white carpet while I cower in the corner. (Well, *cower* might be a strong label here. Perhaps *watch on bravely while whimpering at high alert* is more accurate.) The soil is stubborn. Madden moves a table and covers the soil art I made.

"Do you think she'll notice?" Madden says, looking at the table now standing in the middle of the living room.

Absolutely, I say, proud of our teamwork. *She will love how we've redecorated the place.*

At last Madden gets my blue leash off a hook. I can't stand it anymore, and I get so excited I put my booty on the small piece of carpet near the door and *scootch scootch scootch* until Madden whispers, "Zeus, *no!*"

I stop midscootch, back left paw hovering in the air. *What?*

Madden scowls at me. Scowls are smelly like cow pies. He picks up the rug and takes *forever minutes* to put it in the spinny water machine humans call the *washer.* That thing growls like a monster. At last he returns, sighs, and clips the leash onto my vest. Out we go!

I soon forget about the smelly scowl because *walk!* The air is chilly enough that our breath poofs, and the sidewalk is cold beneath my paw pads. The world today smells metallic, like frosty earth and crystal ice and—oh! There's apparently a cat nearby who likes to use the neighbor's flower bed as his litter box. I make a mental note to return later to terrorize him. From a distance, of course, because claws.

Walk! I get so excited my back feet start moving faster than my front feet, and I scuttle *sideways* until I can get those back paws of mine to obey.

Madden chuckles, and the sound is like the tinkling of the xylophone in band earlier today. And he must start thinking about band, too, because he says, "You know what, Z? My mom made me get you in exchange for being in band. She says band is stressful. *Rigorous* is her word, actually. And if I want to be a part of it, I had to 'be better about managing my diabetes.'" He says this last part in a stiff voice, hard like cardboard, and he waggles two of his fingers up and down as he does.

Rigorous. I like that label. It sounds important. But it sounds like it has claws, too.

"Yeah, she says with something as physical as band, I need to be *vigilant*"—more wagging fingers—"about my health. 'If you're not going to calibrate your CGM, you get the dog.'" He says this in the stiff voice again, and it reminds me of the sound of sandpaper scraping against wood back in the prison workshop.

"And can I let you in on a secret?" Madden asks.

Well, I don't know . . . I begin, because service dogs are by nature blabbermouths, and we find it very hard to keep secrets. But Madden presses on: "I actually chose the tuba because it's the hardest and the heaviest and no one thought I could do it."

Madden smirks. "So it was either *you* or promise to wear a fanny pack stuffed with gear and snacks and stuff. You won over the fanny pack, Z. Congratulations."

My jowls pull into a wide smile. I've never heard of a panny fack, but I can tell I've defeated a formidable foe.

My nostrils perk. Twitch.

Is that . . .

It is!

Ducks.

We round a few more corners, and there it is: a shimmering stretch of glassy pond, covered with a thin layer of gorgeous green icy scum. And on the far shore, huddled in a cloud of stink and poo and feather dander: *ducks.*

I stiffen. Madden unclips my leash. My heart races, and I think back to the drum in band. Why do I keep thinking about stupid band when there's *walk*? Madden looks at me, jerks his head. "Go ahead. Run."

My skin twitches. I shiver. *I . . . can't.*

Madden's eyebrows tighten and his scent washes into a wave of frustration, like a sausage treat that is *juuuuuust* out of reach. "Go on, Z. Run!"

I can't!

A whimper-whine rises in my throat. *Stop being such a puppy, Zeus,* I tell myself. But I can't help it. A high-pitched cry squeaks out of me.

Madden crosses his arms. Narrows his eyes.

I flatten my ears. Narrow my eyes.

Then, at last, he gets it. "Oh, your vest!" He unclips the red cloth I've been wearing since my bathroom break at school, and the moment that third clip is loosened, I wriggle free and push off my back paws and *roofroofroof* around the edge of the pond, breaking through thin glassy ice at points, straight into the cloud of ducks.

WHAT? WHO? YOU! YOU! YOU! NO! They honk at me.

Here's the thing about ducks: I don't want to catch them. They're horrible creatures, what with their waxy bills and weird feet. Plus, feathers taste like a mouthful of sand. But the ducks don't know that. So I *roofroofroof* and they toss cuss words over their shoulders at me (ducks are foul fowl) and they paddle out to the middle of the pond. If the water were warmer, I'd chase them in. Instead I just leap and bark and splash and sneezesneezesneeze—*choo! choo!*—because sometimes the joy can't get out any other way except through nostril explosions.

Madden picks up rocks and starts chucking them sideways at the surface of the pond like Frisbees. Some of them skip across the surface—*plip plip ploop!*—before sinking. Some slide across the thin film of ice and skid to a rest on top. Both are infuriating—how am I supposed to retrieve *those?*

You throw, I fetch—don't you know how this game works, Maddening?

The icy breeze blows a very specific scent across my nose—sweet, like lollipops. My ears perk. I stand straighter.

That smell: it's Madden.

His blood is too sweet.

I race back around the edge of the pond, and the closer I get to him, the more I can smell it: Yes, definitely too sweet. Thick, like honey. I need to alert him.

Madden pauses in his rock-chucking suddenly, and I can smell his demeanor change. "Oh!" He lifts a corner of his shirt, twice pumps a button on the box attached to his belly. I can smell the chemicals stream into his body, mixing with his blood. It's salty. It smells like beef jerky. But it's doing what it's supposed to do. It's making his blood less sweet.

I reach him just as he plops onto a bench. I pant. He looks me in the eyes.

"Did you know?" he whispers, his breath a cloud.

Know what? I feel like I don't know anything about this human.

"Hmph. It coulda been just a fluke. I don't know that you actually knew my blood sugar was high."

Oh, that? Yes, of course I knew.

Madden sits back, sighs. "Mom would wring my neck if she knew I bolused without testing my exact levels, but I didn't bring my test kit."

Ring his neck? It sounds like another band instrument. Like a painful, awful band instrument.

Madden turns to me with of look of . . . pity? Pity is the *worst*, as awful as drinking salt water. "See, Zeus? I *felt* that. That sugar high—I knew my blood was getting out of whack. That's what I mean. I don't really need you. I don't need anyone. See?"

Of course I *see*; I have two eyes. Do I understand? Absolutely not. He felt his blood sugar climbing that time, sure. But what about the next time, or the next, or the next? What about the times it climbs so fast he never feels it coming, and *wham!*

I don't like to think about what happens after *wham*.

Madden scoops up my vest from the dry grass and clips it on, *click click click*. He clasps my leash into the metal ring on my back. I bark a teasing *Bye-bye, birdies* over my shoulder at the ducks. The ducks honk obscenities back at me. Rude.

Madden smells like he's thinking a lot of thoughts, like a pot of stew simmering. Almost boiling. He sits back down on the bench.

"I didn't really know my dad," he says at last, and the thought feels like a meteor crashing to earth, all weighty and fiery. (I know all about meteors thanks to the astronomy class Dave and I took in prison. It was an embarrassing class because I thought the label for the rock that the teacher showed us was *meatier*. Let's just say I pooped pebbles for weeks.)

"My old man," Madden continues. "The only thing he ever gave me is diabetes." He chuckles at that, but it's a plastic chuckle. There he is, being plastic again. That can't be his label, *plastic*. It can't.

"Seriously, though, I don't remember him at all. He died a long time ago." Madden smells bittersweet when he talks about his dad. Like . . . like something I can't *quite* place. "Sometimes I feel like I remember him, but I think those might be stories other people have told me."

Just today in Language Arts, the Glorious Study of Labels, I learned about a thing called *tense*. It means *when things happen*. The way Madden's talking, I

58

know his dad is in the *past tense.*

And I get it. My dad is in the past tense, too. He was at Canine College when I was a pup, but he moved on. He works far away now, doing important scent work for the FBI. My bloodline of bloodhounds is long and impressive. (*Bloodhounds* isn't entirely accurate. We're all German shepherds, me and my relatives.) But Madden's past tense somehow feels more *past*, and definitely more *tense.* Anyway, we have that in common. I know how *past tense* feels.

Past tense feels like missing, like longing, like a favorite tennis ball thrown over a tall fence.

"When I first got diagnosed, Z, I stayed in the hospital for four days. I was nine. I hated needles so much. They made me practice giving shots on an orange. I stuck that thing so many times! Juice was all over me, for days. Even got in my eyes. Man, that hurts! So sticky and sweet—*ugh.* I still hate orange juice. *Hate* it."

I think about that label, *hate.* It smells slick and angry and green.

"Anyway, since then I've been stuck with millions of needles, I'd guess. Test kits and glucose monitors and insulin pumps—all needles. And I've been okay."

Now there's a label that smells positively bland: *okay.* Like ice. And I feel *okay,* too. I didn't actually *help* Madden, just now. He realized his blood was too sweet all on his own. I've been with him almost one full day now, and so far, the only thing I've done is listen to him. That doesn't seem helpful at all.

"So I don't really see how you're gonna be any better at this than those things, Zeus. I mean, how can an animal beat science and technology? Plus, you are freaking HUGE and really obvious and a lot of work. No offense."

Oh, I take *offense*.

Off. Opposite of *on*. Sometimes yelled at a dog to keep them away from the good furniture.

Fence. A terrible outdoor wall that keeps dogs from running fast like the wind.

So basically, taking *offense* means I feel terrible, like I've been yelled at, penned in.

Madden shakes his head. "But diabetes really stresses my mom out. I mean, I get it . . ."

His voice drifts off. His scent flutters back to the bittersweet smell he wears when he talks about his dad, and I realize what it smells like: the musky smell of a dandelion wish as it's carried away on the wind. He blinks. "If having you around means I finally get to do the stuff that all the other kids do, like band . . ."

Again, he doesn't finish his sentence. I sniff harder,

trying to figure out what those two sentences floating off together might mean.

"So yeah. I don't need you or want you, Zeus, but I'm stuck with you."

Stuck. That word feels awful, like gum in fur. My head hangs. My tail tucks. I'm *stuck* with Madden.

Madden stands again. He picks up my leash and we head toward our bleachy-clean home. I think back over what Madden said, and I realize: Madden and his mom aren't exactly the best of chums. They play tug-of-war constantly: they grumble and circle and tug to and fro.

Which is usually great, except in this game, I'm the rope.

★ 8 ★

I BROKE THE HIKERS

Maddening: when we get back to the house, Madden's mom asks, "How was the walk?" and he just grunts and leads me upstairs. In his room, I sit on his bed and watch the orbs spinning on his ceiling while he finishes his homework. Their movement is like the poetry our Language Arts teacher Mr. Nance recites: round floaty words that slip past one another, silent and circular. The whole thing feels almost too big to label, but the word *home* keeps swooping through my noggin.

My eyes get heavy. Droop.

Madden nods at me. "Me too, bud. Let's go to bed."

Last night, I slept on a new, stiff dog bed in the

62

corner of Madden's room. The tags are still sewn into it, and they are crinkly and uncomfortable, like sleeping on poking fingers. The thing smells like a factory, too, like the poofy white fuzz I love to rip out of toys. It is too small for me.

So when Madden points to the too-tiny pallet and says, "Bed, Zeus," I don't jump down. My heartbeat speeds and my mouth gets dry and my paw pads sweat—I am being *disobedient*! But I'm so tired after this first full day, and I want to sleep *here*, in the big human bed. Madden sighs and shoves me to the side (I grunt, pretending to protest) and crawls in beside me.

Yes! I smile, my tongue lolling. *I won!* The Battle of the Bed. I am legendary, and puppies will study my tactics for years to come.

We sleep. I dream of ducks, and I feel myself *twitch!* They cuss and poop. Silly fowl.

My dream turns to Madden, and I imagine him floating on a raft in the middle of the ocean, fingers dipping into the sea. He lifts and lifts and lifts, curling into the arc of a huge wave. I startle awake.

My nostrils perk.

It's Madden. He snores lightly next to me, and his blood is too salty and falling fast. He is awash in salt, drowning in an ocean.

I nudge him. Nothing.

I nudge harder, press my cold, wet nose on his cheek. He grunts, swipes at the smudge I left behind, and rolls over. His scent darkens, a sea wave curling over our heads.

Wake up, Madden!

I leap off the bed, bite the corner of his blanket, and tug, tug, tug. Madden yanks back but remains asleep. The wave tightens its curl around us . . .

Wake UP, Madden!

I shake, rattling my tags to get his attention, and realize with a start that I can make music! But even that doesn't stir him.

I want to bark, and I even feel grumbling in my belly. One huge, bellowing bark would do the trick. But I'm a *service dog*. Since we can't bark when we are in public, we are trained to *never* do it to get our human's attention. Barking is for show-offs. It is *obvious*. My dad always said so.

My eyes scan the dark, shadowy room for something that might wake him up. Then I see it: the hikers!

I reach my paw out, sigh heavily, and *tap!* I knock the photo over.

It crashes to the floor, the glass in the frame shattering.

I broke the hikers.

Madden sits up with a start, as if a part of *him* were

64

shattering. He looks bleary, confused, and I know it's not just from being sleepy—his blood is way too salty.

"Zeus, *no*!"

But I don't have time to feel ashamed, to tuck my tail and wind into a small ball. I lick his hands. Nudge him again. I can *taste* how salty his skin is.

"Do I need to check?" he asks. I lick him, *Yes!*

Madden pulls a black cloth case from beneath his pillow. He zips it open. Dozens of smears of blood coat the inside of the case. He pulls out a thing—a small tool that looks like a screwdriver—and staples the side of his finger, *caCHUNK*. The noise is loud in the quiet room.

I circle and pace, pace and circle as Madden squeezes a dark red drop of blood onto a tiny piece of paper, then slides the paper inside a small black box. A blue screen on the box lights up. Madden has a lot of black boxes with blue screens in his life. So far I've counted three.

"Sixty-five?" Madden says, blinking. "Wow. That's low." His blood needs more sugar. He reaches under his bed, grabs his basket of snacks, and pops five gummy bears in his mouth. I circle and pace, pace and circle.

Madden's murky vision washes off him like the sea pulling backward into itself, and his eyes clear. He grabs another of his black boxes, scans a small plastic patch attached to his upper arm. More plastic.

Beep! Madden studies the screen on this black box, the blue light washing over his face. "Huh. My CGM says I'm fine. Says eighty-two. I wonder why it didn't pick up that low?"

He looks at me, circling and pacing. His blood is starting to sweeten, but I can't sit. Not yet. He's swimming toward the shore, but he's not safe yet. I'll tackle him and drag him to safety by his pajama collar if I have to.

Madden puts all his devices and snacks away and leaps out of bed. He lifts the photo of the hikers off the floor. He gingerly removes the photo from the brokenness and tosses the frame in his garbage can. He dusts shards of glass off the hikers' smiles.

"She told them to stay away, Zeus," he whispers, more to the photograph than to me. His eyes are suddenly glassy. "Mom told Nana and PopPop that we needed 'time to get to know each other again.'" The way he says this, I picture him doing that thing where he wiggles two fingers on each hand, but he doesn't do it. He's too tired, too recently washed ashore.

"Man, they love music, Zeus. Nana and PopPop. Pops was in a band just for fun. Played all sorts of gigs, like weddings and bar mitzvahs. He used to take me along to help. And Nana played this silly green ukulele all the time." He chuckles, but it's a sad laugh. "She's an awful musician, but she loves music more than any-one I know. Sings all the time. If you can call it singing. Their house was full of music, Z. Not quiet like here."

He's silent a bit, then glances at me. "That could've been another coincidence, you know. Your nudging. That wasn't necessarily an alert." He tucks the photo under his pillow, pulls the blanket over his head, and immediately falls into a deep sleep.

Coincidence? Hmph! I happen to know that *coincidence* is a fancy human word for *lucky*, and there's nothing lucky about my training.

I circle, I spin, I pace, until at last Madden smells right. He's safely anchored ashore. And he has no idea how close he was to getting pulled out to sea.

I hop back onto Madden's bed.

I take all the pillows and stretch out my legs fully, shoving Madden way over to one side, almost dropping him off the side of the bed. Almost, but *not quite.*

Not quite. As maddening as he is, I won't let him drop.

★ 9 ★

OPERATION DESTROY MUSIC IS A SUCCESS

A middle school cafeteria contains every human smell there is: Food, all kinds. Cleaning products. Bodies. Soap and deodorant. Burps and farts. Feet. And most important: Madden's blood. Madden's medicine.

It is an assault on my nose, all these smells at once. I can only lie at Madden's feet and pant, tasting all of it. Being able to taste smells is usually awesome, but not here. I smack my jaws and keep panting.

Bits of food rain down around me, because middle schoolers apparently have bad aim and miss their mouths a lot. If they had a big jaw like me, that wouldn't be a problem. I never miss a bite of kibble. Never.

A sliver of fried potato falls directly on my paw. I am

68

not supposed to eat in my vest, and the lieutenant said I couldn't eat human food. It would be *disobedient*, but it is right there. I slide my eyes around: nothing but feet, feet, feet, noise, noise, noise. My tongue darts from my mouth and *slurp!* Bye, potato. Ah, human food.

Disobedience tastes salty and greasy.

Madden sneaks his hand to the black box under his shirt and gives himself two pumps of medicine. He doesn't even look when he does it. He is not supposed to give himself his medicine this way. He is supposed to test the level of his blood sugar first with a finger staple, and then calculate a proper dosage of medicine from there. But that is obvious, and it takes a few minutes. I close my eyes and try to sort through the scents, try to focus on just those two smells: blood and medicine. He is in range. He is *okay*.

We stand. "No shake, Zeus," Madden commands. I know he tells me this so I won't shimmy after a long time sitting and fling my fur all over this food cave.

Dude, I say. *These people eat ketchup on pizza. You really think they'll notice a tiny bit of fur?*

In Language Arts, we study a poem written by a woman named Emily about her cat:

She sights a Bird—she chuckles—
She flattens—then she crawls—

She runs without the look of feet—
Her eyes increase to Balls—

I huff-puff loudly. Runs without the look of feet? Who looks at their feet when they run? No one, that's who, *Emily*. Hmmph. Cats. They get all the glory.

And then: band!

It is time to keep Madden from being *outstanding*.

We walk into the room, and it smells like spit and oil and the musty curves of old brassy instruments. The ingredients for music.

An eighth-grade trumpet player named Jesus points a mouthpiece at us and says, "Hi, Madden. Hey, Zeus!" Then he flips the mouthpiece between his fingers and points it at himself: "'Hey, Zeus' from Jesus—get it? *Ha!*"

Oh, I understand. He says my name with a *hey*, so our names sound the same. Human humor. I love him—Jesus. I wag to let him know.

The students get settled: *Scrape! Bang! Blam! Tweet!*

I scan the busy room: music stands and black instrument suitcases and chairs and a large podium at the front and a desk off to the side and *aha!* There!

I can smell it from here: a hot, inky stack of papers sitting on the corner of Mrs. Shadrick's desk, all with birds on them. Target acquired.

70

Mrs. S writes something on the whiteboard, *squeak squeak*, while the kids settle like leaves beneath a tree. The symbols she draws today aren't birds. They're fat circles, like lazy bumblebees humming over the wires:

Music is all about the birds and the bees, I suppose.

Mrs. S turns, rubs the palms of her hands together, and smirks.

"Pop quiz! We're playing F-minor scales today, kids."

"Nooooooo!"

"Aw man!"

"Crap. The one scale I didn't practice."

Mrs. S cracks her knuckles and tries to look like a villain, but I can tell she's not really one. "Who wants to begin? Ashvi?"

My tail thumps at the mention of her name. Ashvi lifts her flute to her bottom lip. Her music flitters forth, and this thing that she plays, the F scale? It somehow reminds me of a skeleton. It is the bones of music. I picture the bones waking, stretching, and tiptoeing up a flight of stairs. The skeleton then pivots and skips lightly back down the steps to where it started.

It is lovely, her Ashvi music. I wish it weren't lovely, but it is: light and flittery and swoopy. It's much easier to destroy something that's dark and greasy and heavy instead of something as splendid as music.

Ashvi finishes her scales. Her last note hovers above us like a hummingbird. Madden glows yellowy soft like a dandelion.

Then a rumbling begins, and my first thought is, *Earthquake!* A green cloud of foot stink rises from the floor. I realize: the students are stomping their feet. And *then* I realize: this is like applause, like tail-wagging, only these humans can't use their hands because they're all holding instruments. They're stomping their feet instead. And even though the stink of this stomping makes my eyes water, it's ingenious, and I smile because sometimes humans are really smart, and my tail wags, and I tell them, *I love you, humans!*

Mrs. S smiles. "That was excellent, Ashvi. Go grab a snack out of the treasure chest for that one."

Ashvi lowers her instrument into her case, hops up, and crosses to a box at the front of the room. "Twizzlers—YES!" she mutters.

The students continue playing the F scales: a

trumpet here (after emptying the spit valve—practical but gooey), a trombone there (like watching spit rain. I wonder if perhaps music comes from saliva).

Jake plays his scales. Mrs. S says he "nailed it," and Jake leans over and mutters to Madden, "Yeah, I did."

They're all distracted with their bumblebee notes and their stomping feet and their revenge.

Time for Operation Eat Sheet. (Sheet music, that is.)

I *drag* my leash over to Mrs. S's desk, scan the room. No one heard that. I'm sure of it.

I paw the stack of paper to the floor. No one saw that. I'm sure of it.

I chew.

My heart races. I am saving Madden from certain destruction!

Paper tastes like dry leaves, but my teeth sink into the stack, and I chew, chew, chew as fast as I can before anyone can spot me. My saliva is magic, too, it seems, because the stiff paper loosens and becomes a gooey, inky mush. Chewing is the most satisfying thing there is—jaw working, saliva flowing . . . I'm smiling and chewing, chewing and smiling.

I gag a bit—*kak*. Too much paper.

My gaze locks with Ashvi's.

Her coppery eyes widen. *Zeus, no!* she mouths. Shakes her head.

I curl. Tuck my tail. Ashvi's eyes dart toward the garbage can, and I can tell she's trying to puzzle out how to throw away the paper I'm chewing without anyone else seeing us.

Ah, the evidence! I try to hide the mush I've created by lying on top of it. There! They won't notice.

A hand slices the air like a bolt of lightning.

Jake's hand.

"Mrs. Shadrick?" he shouts above the saxophone now playing. "Look at Zeus!"

He turns his lightning bolt hand toward me, his pointy finger zapping me all the way across the room.

The saxophone stops playing.

The music screeches to a halt.

All eyes turn on me.

There is complete silence.

Silence?

I've done it!

Operation Destroy Music is a success.

★ 10 ★

TAKE THAT, TUBA

The look Mrs. Shadrick turns on me makes me think of canned dog food: Flat. Bland. Lumpy. No bite.

Her shoulders droop, and I can see the weight she carries on them: teaching all these kids all these instruments, all these notes, all this music. But then she sighs, shrugs, and she's apparently fine managing that weight. She is *business*, and she is awesome. I hate that I have to destroy something she is so good at. "I'll just make more copies of our new sheet music tonight. Zeus, take your seat."

Business. She talks to me like any of her other pupils, and for that, I am grateful. I weave back through the maze of chairs and music stands, but I tuck my tail farther and tighter as I go. The other pupils stare at me, some full of pity, some full of displeasure, and all these eyes on me? It feels like getting poked with the jabby ends of a hundred broomsticks. The glare that pokes the hardest is Ashvi's. Even from across the room, I can smell her disappointment.

I finally reach Madden's chair. The look *he* gives me is angry, like a bee sting. *You're welcome*, I say, trying to lighten things up. I wink at him through all this silence. *Now we can get back to being invisible.* Madden doesn't smile.

"Okay, then. Let's practice 'Feliz Navidad' next," Mrs. S says. The kids fan through the pages in their notebooks, raise their instruments, and *breathe*.

A song skips and bounces out of each instrument.

I blink.

I cock my head.

They can still make music!

And it's as glorious as running wild and fast and free as the wind.

This confuses me. How can I destroy the wind?

I realize my folly: I didn't destroy *all* the sheet music. Each pupil's notebook is filled with sheets, all printed with telephone wires and blackbirds. I can't chew that much paper! The only thing I've seen chew *that* much paper is the terrible copy machine in the front office.

The song bounds and hops around the room like the cats we studied, twitching their whiskers, shimmying their tails. Somehow, the kids look at those pieces of paper and spin the markings into music. Some kind of magic must be involved in that, like dust motes dancing in slanting sunlight, or butterfly wing powder. The students read those blackbirds, hooked and hanging, and then blow into shiny horns, and pound on loud drums, and twee into thin flutes, and altogether it braids rainbows and spins starlight.

I shake my head, jangle my tags. Music is too powerful to label. That scares me. Labels help me understand things, and to understand a thing is to love it.

That's why I haven't yet shouted, *I love you!* to Madden. I can't label him. I don't understand him.

Madden smiles and bounces behind his instrument, beaming like light, his fiery anger forgotten. His blood is wild: up and down, down and up. Not dangerous—not yet—but it's practically dancing, led by the strain of playing music. Madden is anything but invisible right now. Mrs. S shouts, "Nice job, tubas! Keep it up!"

The box over Mrs. Shadrick's head crackles in the middle of the song, and the voice—the Big Dog in the Sky—shouts, "MRS. SHADRICK, MADDEN NEEDS TO TAKE THE BUS AGAIN TODAY."

Madden's gaze bounces in my direction, and I can feel him having to make the choice again between the tuba and me.

And my mission failed. Taking out sheet music wasn't the wisest tactic. There must be a better maneuver, another way to destroy their song. And it must be destroyed; it is too powerful. And it is not good for Madden; I agree with the lieutenant on that. She may have been *reassigned*, but she is correct that the tuba is a big strain on Madden and his blood. Feeling my racing heart, my muscles twitching to the rhythm, my jangling tags, I am more convinced than ever: I must eliminate music.

He chose me again!

Take *that*, tuba.

I've decided to name Madden's brassy, twisted tuba *Beef*, because it reminds me so much of the brassy, twisted Beef I went to school with. Madden leaves Beef behind, and I follow him to the bus. I curl up under the plastic seat in front of Madden.

Herky-jerky, start-and-stop, this bus ride. We wind and turn and bump and it feels like my stomach can't keep up with the rest of me.

Even from under the seat, I can smell Madden's house—*my* house?—approaching, bleachy and strong.

I stand, follow Madden down the aisle, off the bus, onto the cold sidewalk.

"Hey, you!"

It's a voice from the bus. Madden and I turn. A jumble of boys hangs out of various windows overhead. Jake from band is one of them. I don't know why he called Madden *you*. He knows his name.

"You. Is that a seeing-eye dog? Are you blind?"

Madden's mood darkens, turns spicy like a huff of pepper.

"Yes," Madden says calmly. "In fact, I can't even see what finger I'm holding up."

Madden shows the boys one of his fingers.

The bus explodes with a mixture of laughter, gasps, shoving, "*Duuuuude*s," and a few threats of "You're gonna be in so much trouble!" and "Bro, your mom is *right there*." The bus drives away in a blur of noise.

That is one powerful finger.

Someone clears their throat behind us.

The lieutenant!

Madden swirls about. He's embarrassed now, like he got caught sneaking extra treats. This moment feels charged, our hair practically standing on end, just before the lightning.

But instead of her being angry like Madden expects, a small grin blooms on the lieutenant's face. Her eyebrows lift. "Do you hang out with that boy? Jake?"

Madden's mood smells suddenly dry and acrid, like moldy bread. "Not really. We're in band together."

"Yeah? He's my superior's son."

Madden looks and sounds like he is choking on a chicken bone—*kak!* "Really? Your boss is Jake's dad?"

"My superior officer, yes. They seem a lot alike. So how was your day? Is Zeus helping?"

Ah, here we go. Here's where he brags about me at last. How Ashvi talked to Madden for two whole minutes in the hall today, thanks to me shooting her my *hello, there* eyes. How I managed to halt the music momentarily, creating a hollow, echoing silence. How I woke him in the middle of the night and saved him from washing into the inky black sea.

But Madden is maddening.

"Nah, not really."

We go inside, Madden's mom asking about things like carbs and insulin and bolus. Madden mutters, sputters, heads upstairs, slams a door, and starts studying for a test. I follow. I remember tests from my service dog training, so I don't interrupt. I sit in a corner and pull the white, plasticky fluff out of a chew toy. It looks like delicious cotton candy, but it tastes dry and fake.

It tastes maddening.

★ 11 ★

NOT PLASTIC

*S*trict.

I like this human label, and not just for the obvious reason that it sounds a lot like *stick*. (*Stick!*) No, *strict* is a short leash—*strict* keeps you focused. It is a command like *sit* or *stay*, a pinched treat held *juuuuuust* above your wet nose saying, *Look, Zeus!* Middle school schedules are *strict*. The horrible bells shriek a command: *Change classes now!* And the students obey. They follow this strict schedule for six classes every day.

But today! There was a surprise awaiting us in Language Arts: a colorful, plastic jar on each desktop. When the students saw them, their moods grew lighter, fuzzier, sunnier, and they became a pile of shoving, warm, roly-poly puppies.

Now, I like surprises as much as the next dog, which is to say: they are awful and I hate them. Surprises usually involve noise and fire and too-rapid heartbeats. Honestly, why do anything out of the ordinary? But seeing Madden's mood shift from oniony green weed to sunny yellow dandelion makes me smile.

"Nothing says Shakespeare like bubbles, kids!" the teacher, Mr. Nance, announces. "Open your books to page eighty-six. Open your bubble juice—is it called juice? No one's been able to tell me all day. Anyway, I read, you blow. GO!"

And then Mr. Nance, sporting a bow tie and a pair of glasses, hops about the room and recites a poem from memory: "'Double, double, toil and trouble. Fire burn and cauldron bubble!'"

And the kids take out their tiny plastic sticks and *blow*. They breathe out, exhale, and once again, their human breath creates magic.

Orbs! Shiny, clear, plastic orbs, trembling and floating and spinning. Like the orbs that hang in Madden's room. Like, like . . . *music notes*. Madden calls them *bubbles*.

The bubbles drift and shift, round rainbows, all sheen and spin, and each one hovers there, taunting me, tempting me like slow-motion tennis balls. Lovely and confounding, just like music. Drat those music notes, always besting me!

Beautiful and *almost* invisible—my favorite quality in a thing.

My every hair prickles.

A shiver runs down my spine.

My teeth itch.

I whimper a bit.

And then I can't stand it anymore.

I *leap.*

I chomp.

It's fragile, this music bubble, and it bursts before my jaws even close. And—*ugh*—music tastes terrible! And squeaky, like bathtime.

But I can't stop, and now, the students are laughing and cheering me on: "Get 'em, Zeus!" "Catch those bubbles!" My mouth froths, and it's difficult leaping and snapping with my vest and leash. I want to admit defeat, and just when I'm about to surrender, Madden laughs, and his heart makes a sudden tiny *ping!* like a xylophone. His laugh sounded that way yesterday, too. Plastic can't make a sound like that; only warm shiny metal can swell through all the other human noises like a bell.

This is a hint at his label.

I turn to him and smile, bubble juice dripping off my jowls. Madden chuckles and smiles back. Smiles at ME, the one he is stuck with! Maybe he is even starting to like me? His glasses are cleaner today, which means I can see his eyes. *Almost . . . labeled . . .*

But then the terrible, awful demon bell rings, and students do exactly what they're commanded to do: they drop everything, pick up their books, and move to the next thing. Strict.

My paws are slick and sticky from this bubble juice, and in the hallway, I slip on the linoleum floor, but I'm happy because I know one thing for sure: Madden's label is not *plastic.*

As I make my way through the school by Madden's side, guilt suddenly sizzles through me like a too-sunny sidewalk. What I did back there was the *opposite* of invisible! My dad's voice echoes through my skull: *Be invisible like your tail, Zeus.* Oh, I've shamed him. I've shamed *me*! I let my excitement over those silly floating spheres get the best of me. I should've known from the bathy taste of them that they were bad news. I am too late to be invisible in the past tense. But I renew my vow: *From now on, I will be as invisible as my tail.*

And now I have a blankie! *Ahem,* I mean, um, yes, a blanket. In band, Mrs. Shadrick put a wool blanket on the floor for me, and I love it so much I can't wait to shed all over it. Madden burns a bit when she walks over to us and points it out, because this is something else out of the ordinary, something else not invisible. But a blanket! That's not too obvious, right? It has red and black squares and smells like cinnamon rolls.

"I think Zeus was trying to get off our cold floor, chewing up all those papers," she says. "Want to try it out, Zeus?"

Do I! I hop on the blanket and I spin spin spin left, curl, turn turn turn right, march a bit, finally find the spot, and *flop!* Ahhh. This blanket is far better than the hard floor, where all the musicians drain their instruments' spit valves. I smile. My tail thumps.

Jake scowls as always when he has to step over me to get to his chair, and his mood flushes bitter like dark tea. Madden gulps, and his face shifts into a false grin. He points to Jake's shirt. It has a picture of a tuba and words on it.

"'Don't Suck'—ha!" Madden says, pointing at the shirt. He's nervous for some reason. Nervousness smells fruity-sweet and jiggly, like Jell-O. "Good one, Jake."

"Wore it for you, Malone."

Madden's jaw tightens so much I fear he might crack a tooth.

"All right, class," Mrs. Shadrick says, tapping her

stick. (*Stick!*) "Let's play warm-up three." She flips the switch on the *tick tick tick* machine, the one Madden calls a metronome. "Aaaand one—two—ready—play!"

Mrs. Shadrick waves her stick about, and I follow it with my eyes. My heart speeds, and I suppress a whimper. When is she going to throw that thing?

Hummmmmmmmnnn hummn hummn!

The music rises in three long, breathy hums. Mrs. Shadrick shouts, "Bring down your pitch a bit, trombones! You sound high."

Hmmmmmmmmnnn hmmn hmmn!

Three more long, powerful hums overtake the room. Mrs. Shadrick twitches her wrist, and she points the stick at the clarinets. "Make sure you know where you're going, woodwinds." The notes climb higher, brighter, like a yellow bird against a blue sky.

"One more!" Mrs. Shadrick shouts with another flick of the stick. She points it at the xylophone player. "Bring us home, Benjamin!" The notes climb higher still. It is a bird that circles overhead without once flapping its broad wings, flying ever further and lighter.

Tiiiiiinnnggggg tinnnggggg tinggg!

My heart wraps around these three notes, and I feel warm and tingly and zingy and scared because I don't understand where all this *emotion* is coming from. I shake my head to clear it of such nonsense. Emotion makes staying invisible very difficult.

The memory of my father's bark echoes again through my head: *Tails are invisible, Zeus. You turn, it's gone. Be your tail.*

Be my tail. Be my tail. Be my tail.

I'm not doing a very good job at being a tail end.

The warm-up finishes, and Mrs. Shadrick keeps her stick aloft until the sky-high music fades like a sunset. She lowers her stick at last.

Her *stick*!

It controls all of this! All these firework-filled notes, all these starlight tones. *The stick!*

"That's really good sound," Mrs. Shadrick says with a smile. "It sounds like one person, doesn't it?" The earthquake of stomping feet begins, the applause from kids holding instruments.

"Okay, let's jump into practicing 'Sleigh Ride' for the holiday concert." While the kids flip pages of sheet music in their notebooks, Mrs. Shadrick says, "Remember, no extraneous noise during a concert. This means no toe tapping. Bob your heels if you need to keep the rhythm."

Mrs. Shadrick raises her mighty, all-powerful stick, and the music bounds forth like a herd of deer leaping crisscross over a highway. It's messy, fussy—stray music notes blart out *Gerplat! Splote! Flerp!*

Mrs. S frowns. "Jake," she shouts over the melody. "Did your instrument practice itself this week?"

Jake's mood flushes like a toilet. Madden suppresses a grin behind his mouthpiece, his tuba brighter and peppier than before, but his blood dances wild with his music-making.

Mrs. S slashes the air like a knife with her powerful stick, and the music limps to the side of the highway and dies like roadkill. "That was . . ." she says, and shakes her head. "That needs work. Practice at home, kids. And when you get sick of practicing, practice some more. And then when you're done practicing . . . Hey, I know! Practice."

She sighs. Places her stick down.

Places her stick down. Check.

"Let's do some individual work instead. Madden?"

All eyes turn to Madden. His gaze flicks to Ashvi, then to the front of the room. "Yes, ma'am?"

"G-major scales, please."

Madden clears his throat, lifts his tuba, and plays. It's like watching a bright red cardinal hop to the tip of a snow-coated pine tree, then flit gently back down to its nest. The sugar in his blood dips.

The stomping feet rumble.

"Excellent," Mrs. S says. "Madden, help yourself to the treasure chest."

Madden stands, crosses the room. I follow.

He peers into a plastic chest. It's filled with dusty bags of pretzels and shiny, colorful bits of candy. He pauses.

Mrs. Shadrick picks up a flute and shows one of the students where her fingers should rest. She begins playing it, and all the students smile and watch her create tail-chasing-fast flute music. No one is paying attention to me. This is it!

I *streeeeeetch* my leash as far as I can.

It's not enough.

I *straaaaain* my long neck.

Almost . . . there . . .

I *reeeeeeach* my long, pink tongue out, and *slurp!*

I got it!

I got the stick!

It is chewy and springy between my teeth, but I can't enjoy some full-on chomping right now. I have to hide it. I duck my head, tuck my tail. I am camouflaged this way. *Nice work, son,* I can practically hear my proud parents say.

We cross back to our chairs. Sit.

Jake glares at me with two laser-pointer eyes. His hand twitches like it's about to shoot into the air.

Madden flips a bag of animal crackers over in his hand. "You want these, Jake? I shouldn't eat them."

Jake's eyes slide from me, with Mrs. S's baton tucked between my jaws, and Madden. "Sure."

I slip the baton into Madden's tuba case, tucked beneath some crumpled sheet music. (Stupid sheet music—I haven't forgotten our battle!)

Jake pockets the animal crackers. He looks at me again, eyes narrowed.

I flatten my ears, curl into my blanket. Jake saw me. I know he saw me.

Why didn't he rat me out?

★ 12 ★

I RULE AT STICK!

Today the lieutenant picks us up from school in her rumbling, tall truck, and I get to eat sky and suck gnats up my nostrils the whole way home, and it is glorious. Madden brings his huge tuba suitcase, and after the forever longest and most boring part of the day (homework), he flips the two silver latches on the case—*click click*—and hurls the top open.

You'd think Madden was opening a box of sunshine, the way he glows when he peers inside. The instrument reflects off the sheen of his glasses, and from my angle on the floor, it looks like his eyes are filled with tubas. He traces his fingers lightly over the brassy surface before lifting each section of the tuba out of the case.

He puts a few drops of earthy, pungent oil on the cork that lines the edge of each piece and rubs them in with his finger, then swipes an oily fingerprint across his jeans. He screws the three pieces together to make his instrument. Beef the tuba. *Hmmpf.*

Madden doesn't notice the stick I've hidden in his case. He winces as always when his tuba rests against his insulin pump. He flexes his lips. He adjusts his mouthpiece, places it against his mouth, and *breathes.*

I watch the ice of Madden's day melt off him, like steam curling above frosty grass as the pink sun rises. He smiles inside, and his instrument smiles with him. The tuba is a bouncy, peppy instrument, but low-sounding, like crawling, like sneaking, like the grumbling that might come from your belly. Madden closes his eyes, and it's hard to tell where he ends and his instrument begins.

I sneak the baton out of his case and jump on the bed. I *chew.* Ah, heavens, is there anything more perfect than chewing? This stick has just enough bend to make it a springy bite, but not so soft it crumbles and splinters between my jaws. A solid nine-out-of-ten chew texture. Would chew again.

Madden's song is bouncing and prancing along until *plert!* It sounds like a stumble, a missed step on a staircase. Madden blinks, shakes his head. He backs up a bit in the song and tries again: *plert!* It sounds like the song is cracking in two. His brow furrows. "Ugh. High C. I'll never get this part right."

Now, *that* feeling, I know.

The lieutenant ducks her head in. "I just made an appointment with your endocrinologist. I hope your A1C levels are better than last visit." She lifts her chin at Madden. "How much insulin on board now?"

If Madden was thawing earlier, he flash-freezes when he has to hold the tuba away from his heart to check his insulin pump. "Two and a half units," he mutters.

The lieutenant nods. "Well, don't eat snacks unless you need to. We're having leftovers for dinner."

Leftovers? There is *leftover* food? Why not just eat it all? Sounds to me like leftovers are for quitters.

The lieutenant stands in the doorway. "Anything else?" Madden asks.

"Can you keep the music down? It's a little loud."

She leaves, and Madden's shoulders slump. He disassembles his tuba and gently places it back in its case. "Who wants to go outside?"

Me! I bark. Any question that begins with *who wants to* is usually me, I've noticed. Humans don't ask that of one another. *Me! I do!*

"Shhhh," Madden says to me. "Let's not be too *loud*, right?"

He walks out the door of his room and down the stairs, and I grab the stick and follow. I've enjoyed my chewing, but now it's time to bury the evidence. Literally. There's an excellent digging spot next to the back corner of the fence, and this stick is going right into a big hole.

Madden slides open the glass door and stands faceup in the pale winter sun. His inhale is deep; his exhale is clouds. I can still hear the tuba music his breath makes.

I tiptoe past him, baton in my jaws.

"Hey, Zeus! You found a stick. Who wants to play catch?"

I bark, *Me, I do!*

Then I realize: Oh. Wait. No, I don't. Not with this stick.

But it's *catch*! I can't help myself. I bark again. I hop. *Me! Me! Pick me! I RULE AT STICK!*

Madden picks up the stick, throws it. It flips end over end, my slobber glinting in the soft yellow sun. I dash. I leap. My jaws wrap around the baton, sink deliciously into the wood.

Catch!

I bring the stick back, drop it at Madden's feet. It

flips and arcs; I jump and catch. We do this several times. Madden isn't mad at all! Deep down inside, he must *want* music destroyed. Yes!

Music is the kind of foe that casts spells with its beauty, but I've *almost* defeated it.

I *knew* it. I knew keeping us invisible was the right choice.

I drop the stick at his feet again. He picks it up, but this time, he flips it over in his hand.

"What the—"

His mood grows stormy. "Is this Mrs. S's baton? Zeus, *no*! Bad dog! BAD DOG!"

I sit, then lie.

Bad dog?

Being on the receiving end of a *bad dog* is worse than being jabbed with a broomstick. It's worse than a kick to the ribs. It's worse than doctor needles or gravel roads or long, hot stretches without water.

We've been learning about scales in science, and here's mine, from best to worst:

Whoossa good boy?

Good dog!

Atta boy.

No, Zeus!

Bad dog.

Bad dog is the absolute worst.

Bad dog means I'm failing my human. But I've been doing such a good job destroying music!

Suddenly, I get it. I have a choice: fail my mission or fail my human.

★13★

THE DINGY RAFT

My dreams are filled with the terrible noise of the shrieking bells at middle school, intermixed with the *tick tick tick* of the metronome. *Shriek tick tick. Shriek tick tick.* My muscles twitch, my paws claw at the air, but I can't wake up.

In the dream, I pant and spin. There's Madden, his toes dangling off the edge of a small, dingy raft in the middle of a vast ocean. His legs splash, but there's no ripple in this rollicking sea. The raft lifts and lifts and lifts, then thankfully slides down the backside of a wave. But there is another, bigger wave behind him. There is another, bigger wave behind that.

I jerk awake. Madden's there, asleep beside me.

And the beeping, shrieking sound is coming from one of his black boxes. It sits on his nightstand, glowing and buzzing.

His blood sugar is way too low. It smells as briny and salty as shallow tide pools on a hot summer day. And the bed—it's wet. Urine. It's not unusual for a person with diabetes to urinate while asleep; I learned this in my training. Their bodies are trying to balance things out. But the salty blood? *That's* concerning. The smell is off—way off.

I nudge Madden with my cold nose. Lick his face. Pull the soggy sheets off him, all the way to the end of the bed. The blankets are dotted with tiny drops of blood from the hundreds of times he's pricked his fingers to test his sugar levels. He shivers, but he doesn't wake up.

I'm sorry I chewed the stick, I say. *I'm sorry you had to hide it in the garbage. Please don't be mad at me anymore. Wake up!*

Madden still has the photograph of the hikers tucked under his pillow, so I can't use that to stir him. If only I could bark! But I can't. That's simply not how service dogs do things. *Wake up, Madden!* He needs sugar, immediately.

Sugar!

Madden keeps sugar under his bed in his snack box. I sneak under the low bed (a tight fit, and one of my tall ears gets snagged in the maze of metal underneath. *Yipe!*). I tug tug tug until the box is free.

I dig out a bag of gummy bears, place it next to Madden's head. A box of raisins. Some chewy waxy candies. And then juice boxes. One by one, I pile them around his head. I drop one on his face, and he sputters awake at last.

Madden's vision is cloudy and muddled, I can tell from his blinking. He groans, jams his fingertips against his temples, and says, "Ugh, my head!" He looks around at his bed: wet, stripped of sheets, piled high with sugar. He doesn't even check his black boxes; he fumbles with the straw of a juice box and gulps it down.

His blood almost immediately takes a turn, like watching a raft reach its highest point on a wave, hover there just under the crest for the slightest of moments, then propel forward instead of drowning under the curl of the sea. Whew!

Madden shivers. Gulps. Blinks several more times. At last, he looks at his black boxes. When did it stop beeping and shrieking? "Fifty-two? Why didn't this thing wake me up?"

I pace and pant while I wait for this wild frothy surf to slow. At last, it calms.

After another few blinky foggy minutes, Madden gets a towel from his bathroom and spreads it out over his mattress. He gets a clean blanket and curls up under it. He pushes all the sugar I piled around him to the floor. I suppose he's too groggy to wash his soiled sheets now. Having your blood sugar dip and sway like that can really disorient a person.

The bed is still wet, but I hop up on it, spin a few times, and flop next to Madden. But instead of him curling way off to one side like he usually does, Madden throws a warm arm over my neck and whispers, "Geez, that was scary. Thanks, Z."

And then his heart does it again: it makes a happy tiny *ting!* like the chime of a xylophone.

Huh.

His heart makes music even when the rest of his body shrieks.

The next morning, Madden balls up his sheets and brings them downstairs to the washer. He crams them inside, dumps in powder that smells like fake flowers, and pushes a button. *Whoosh!* The sound of water rushing into the machine fills the room. The washer starts bucking like a wild horse.

Madden turns to me, lays a single finger across his lips. "Don't tell Mom," he whispers. "She'll just worry."

The machine growls. *Worry?* I say. *Yes, I'd worry, too, with a terrible machine like that turned loose in my home.*

★ 14 ★

CHAOS THEORY

The next afternoon there is another surprise (ugh, surprises!) waiting for us in science class: a brightly colored balloon tied to the back of each seat! I grumble, and my fur rankles. Balloons are sneaky things. Quiet, flimsy pieces of plastic, and yet they *move*. Balloons are not to be trusted.

But I can't bark. I stifle my grumblings. *Remember how you embarrassed yourself with those bubbles, Z,* I tell myself. *BE YOUR TAIL.*

Ms. Yang, the science teacher, instructs the kids to untie their balloons. "Okay, kids. Today we're discussing *chaos theory* and how that applies to weather patterns."

Chaos! There's that dastardly word again.

Chaos is a thing I studied with Dave when we were taking our astronomy class in prison. It's how space began: with confusion and bedlam. Atoms and particles and star stuff flinging everywhere—*Kapow! Zip! Zam!* All turmoil and madness until things slowed, cooled, melted together.

And the best way to make sense of chaos? LABELS.

Kids untie their balloons. A student named Jerome rubs his balloon on a girl named Madeleine's hair and makes it stand straight up. Another kid, Davis, tickles his balloon with his fingertips, and it giggles with horrible squeaks. Jake punches his balloon before untying it, *boom boom boom*. Madden chuckles at all this and untangles the knot of his balloon string.

"Okay, okay," Ms. Yang says. "Now. On the count of three, we're all going to release our balloons to the ceiling. What's going to happen? Yes, Madeleine?"

Madeleine's hand is always the first in the air. "They're going to rise."

"Yes, and?"

"Well, I guess . . . they'll rise at the same rate?"

"Yes! What else?"

Madeleine shrugs, and Ms. Yang prompts her. "Will they rise straight up?"

"I think so."

"Let's try it. One, two, three!"

And they release the herd of awful balloons. I don't really know what to expect, because while I know balloons are not alive, they are wily. But they fly to the ceiling much as Ms. Yang said: straight up, mostly all at the same pace. Like a herd of sheep, those things. They hit the ceiling silently and bounce around. They're up to something, those sly balloons. A small whimper escapes me.

"So, yes. The balloons rose at about the same rate, and relatively straight up. This is called *order*." I smile, and my tongue lolls out because I LOVE order! Order is so orderly.

"Okay, now grab the strings and follow me," Ms. Yang says. She pushes open the door to outside, and we all follow, each pupil toting a balloon. The orbs bounce and ping off each other as the students bounce and ping off each other.

We walk to the soccer field and stop. It's a windy day, gray, and the sky stretches like a wide-open yawn.

"Okay. We're going to release these balloons again, and . . . yes, Madeleine?"

"Balloons aren't environmentally safe to release, Ms. Yang."

Ms. Yang smiles. "Ah, but these are! One hundred percent biodegradable. Glad you're thinking about that,

Madeleine. Ten points to Ravenclaw."

Madeleine chuckles and bounces on her toes.

"Okay. When we release the balloons out here, what's going to happen?"

"Chaos, obviously," Jake mutters nearby. A group of his buddies chuckles.

They will rise straight up at the same rate, I answer. I lift my chin. I am a fast learner. Everyone at Canine College said so.

No one answers Ms. Yang other than me, so she smiles. "Well, let's see, then, shall we? One, two, three, *release*!"

AND THIS TIME? Do the balloons rise straight up? Do they rise at the same rate? No and no! They sway. They swirl. They bounce off each other. I can't believe I didn't get the answer right. I watch them dive and dip and dance, and for some reason, I think of music! All those notes, twining and twirling and rising like vines. Bouncing off each other, more beautiful together than separate.

Drat you, music! Get out of my head!

"So, obviously, the balloons aren't rising at the same rate, and they aren't rising straight up. And if we were to release another set of balloons from these exact spots, they would take different paths yet again. Why?"

Every pupil is staring at the lovely tangle of balloons

overhead, dancing ever farther away.

"Wind," Madden says, face turned skyward.

"Yes, and?" asks Ms. Yang. "What other factors might affect their path?"

"Tree branches!"

"The other balloons bouncing into them."

"Telephone wires."

"Rain? Or, you know, moisture in the air we can't see."

"Bugs? And maybe birds?"

"Yes and yes and yes!" Ms. Yang smiles and claps. "There are countless things out here that are making these balloons stray off their path. That's what chaos theory is. It says that sometimes, there are so many things that can affect a situation, the outcome can be nearly impossible to predict."

What? Impossible to predict? Chaos theory sounds terrible. We should go back inside, to order.

"And the farther away those balloons go," Ms. Yang continues, "the harder it is for us to know what might get in their path. Who knows what might throw them off course? Chaos only gets more chaotic."

This feels like it should apply to my life somehow. All these spinning parts, all this *chaos*, pinging against me and my well-laid plans to destroy music. In Language Arts, Mr. Nance calls this a *metaphor*. But I *can't quite* put my paw on what it means.

"That's why weather gets harder to predict the farther out we try. There are too many elements affecting the outcome. The good news is, there *are* patterns in chaos. We can predict some things."

The balloons are so high up and dotty now, I almost fall over watching them. I feel spinny, like I've eaten too much grass. Thinking about chaos and all the things out there stepping in my path? Throwing me off course? I want to whimper.

All the pupils are silent, watching the balloons get gobbled up by the vast yawn of the sky. They all feel the metaphor, too: the chaos of middle school.

How am I supposed to keep Madden invisible when all these unpredictable things—like music—just keep lifting him higher?

★ 15 ★

GUILTIER THAN
AN INDOOR PILE OF . . .

We sneak into the band room. Usually, I would say we "walk in," but if Madden had a tail right now, it'd be tucked tight. He averts his eyes from anyone else's.

Hoo boy! Madden smells guiltier than an indoor pile of . . . you know. I wonder what he did!

"Hey, Zeus!" Jesus says as we take our seats.

Jesus! I wink. Our labels sound the same, and I love him.

Mrs. Shadrick sits at her desk and peers over her glasses. Poor humans, always having to put plastic in front of their tiny eyes to see. "Mr. Malone. Can you come up here for a moment?"

Madden nods and burns crimson red, like those fiery cinnamon candies he eats sometimes when his blood sugar dips. He bites the inside of his cheek, and a whiff of worry wafts from him. His eyes flick to her conductor's stand.

Ah, I see. He is worried about her missing baton, and how to explain that this time, I've officially destroyed music. My chest puffs with pride. Beguiling music: foe no more!

Mrs. S lowers her voice when we get to her desk. "Madden. Do you know what this is about?"

Madden burns so red I expect him to explode and turn into a pillar of ash at any moment. Here is where he explains about there being no more music. "I . . . think so?"

"You gave your prize away yesterday. It never occurred to me that snacks wouldn't be a good reward. But of course they aren't good for you! I can change up the prize system. What do you suggest?"

Madden's eyes dart over his shoulder and around the room, like he's making sure none of his classmates have heard this. He shouldn't worry—if anything is more ineffective than human eyes, it's human ears. "No! I mean—it's okay. Please don't do that."

"Are you sure? Because . . ."

Madden shakes his head so vigorously, I picture

him flinging off droplets of water. "Nah. The others—they really like those snacks. Don't replace them just for me."

Mrs. S nods, and we take our seats. The air now crackles with instrument noise, like a hot summer morning filled with chirruping birds and singing crickets. A peppy theme bounces up from the xylophone like leaves lifted on the wind. A drum *rat-a-tat-tat*s, a woodpecker thrumming. Drumsticks tick against one another. A trumpet *blart*s. A clarinet *twee*s. Cymbals crash like sunflowers smiling.

It is *chaos*, like we learned in science. Noise. Not music, not without the baton.

Mrs. Shadrick knocks her knuckles on her wooden stand to get the pupils' attention. "I want the first, third, and fifth rows only to tune with a partner. Tune by ear."

The pupils partner up. A single, huge hum swells and fills the space, like a tractor motor.

It's working! They are *not* making music!

"Okay, now rows two and four. Tuning only!"

Another hum, higher-pitched but still bland. If sounds had a taste, this one would be a plain cracker, no salt.

I HAVE DONE IT!

Without the baton, the only noise they can make is

flat, like listening to a steamroller for fun. Except it is no fun.

I WIN!

Mrs. S flips on the metronome, *tick tick tick*. "Okay, good. Let's start with 'Song for the Winter Moon' today. Page forty-six. Ready, set, let's PLAY!"

She lifts her hands, flits her fingers.

And they *play*.

The music starts out low, a blackbird asleep in a bush. The bird wakes at midnight and takes flight, sewing herself through beams of moonlight, her black feathers gleaming. *Ting!* goes the triangle, and I can see her darting between pinpricks of stars. *Ting ting!* She swoops, she swirls, the earth (tubas and trombones) low and solid beneath her, the treetops (flutes and clarinets) tickling her wingtips.

"Good, good!" Mrs. S yells, fingers lifting. "Keep going!"

My throat swells. My nose tingles. I do not understand why music makes me feel this way! I do not understand how Mrs. S teases the song from their breath *without the baton.*

They've almost completed the piece, almost tucked the blackbird back into her cozy nest just as the first sunbeam pierces the sky. Mrs. S lifts her hands, lowers them, and the music sleeps.

111

"Excellent!" she says. She turns to the bass sax. "But, Ren, I've heard better from you. It's like you have inches of dust on your instrument case."

The pupil, Ren, blinks from behind his huge instrument. "Huh?"

"Dude. When's the last time you practiced?"

The other pupils titter and giggle. Ren grins and nods. "I'll practice tonight, Mrs. S. Promise."

"Please do. All of you, please practice. That was good, really good, but I know it can be great."

A trombone *flarp*s, and the pupils laugh again. There is a lot of laughter in this room.

Mrs. S smiles. "Nothing like a trombone fart to lighten things up. But remember: at the concert, *no* extraneous noise. Don't even so much as sneeze at this thing, okay, or you *will* need God to bless you once I get ahold of you."

Eli, one of the drummers, slips in a quick *ba-DUM! PEESH!* on his drum and cymbal.

Mrs. S chuckles. "Nice rim shot, Eli. But I mean it. Say it with me, class: ABSOLUTELY NO SNEEZING."

"No sneezing," they intone back with giggles.

"Now," Mrs. S says, rubbing her palms together. "I've decided to assign a duet for the concert."

The class becomes a shifting, wiggling thing, a

bright orange fuzzy caterpillar on a hot sidewalk. My ears twitch toward the whispers:

"A duet?"

"Cool!"

"Aw, man. The triangle is never picked for that kind of thing."

Mrs. S clears her throat and the students calm. "So. Ashvi and Madden, I'd like for you to take those parts, if you're interested?"

Madden?

Oh no!

It's getting *worse*. He is *more outstanding*. This will never do.

But Madden glows like he's just eaten a nest of fireflies. (Do *not* recommend, by the way. Fireflies look as if they'd taste like candy. They do not.) "Sure! Thanks, Mrs. S."

Ashvi smiles over her shoulder at Madden, then pops forward again. "Yes, ma'am. Thank you!"

"Come get your sheet music, then."

While Madden and Ashvi gather their new music, the other pupils *blart* and *blurp* into their instruments. Jake glares at the back of Madden's head, snarls against the twisted gleam of the metal on his teeth, and—*FLEERRRRM!*—blasts his anger through his

113

tuba. It comes out the other end smelling like garlic.

The bell shrieks. Kids click and snap and slam their instruments and cases and lockers. Ashvi hops toward us, and I kid you not: she is prettier than a plateful of shiny sausage. I wag.

"Can I come over to your house to practice?" she asks Madden. His skin melts off his bones into a puddle at his feet again, but Ashvi doesn't seem to notice. "I really want to nail this duet."

"Uh, how about we meet at the pond in my neighborhood instead? Right after school?"

Ashvi smiles starbursts and comets. "Sure. Oh man, we're going to be great together! I'll bring snacks."

Snacks?!

Not *snacks*!

Based on the lieutenant's reaction to snacks, based on Mrs. S wanting to get rid of them just because of Madden, snacks are a terrible, horrible thing.

But Madden mumbles, "Cool, yeah." And Ashvi floats away as if she's on water.

Madden rubs the back of his neck and tries not to smile too big. He picks up his tuba case, his backpack, and my leash, and we head toward the door.

"Mr. Malone? Another word, please?"

We both turn, me and Madden.

Jake is there, next to Mrs. Shadrick, scraping his

dry lips across his metal teeth. It makes him look like a bulldog. I instinctively step in front of Madden.

"Madden," Mrs. S says, and her mood smells as fishy as a dirty aquarium. "Jake here says you stole my baton. Do you know anything about that?"

★ 16 ★

GARBAGE PARTY!

Madden rushes through the front door to the kitchen garbage can, the one that smells like bacon grease and old broccoli and orange peels and eggshells. Heavenly. He peers inside. "No, no, *no*," he mutters. "Uh, Mom?"

The lieutenant answers from upstairs. "Yes?"

"Did you take the garbage out?"

"If you're asking if I did your chore for you, then yes, Madden, I did."

Madden huff-puffs deeply and narrows his eyes at me. My ears twitch. I follow Madden to another, bigger can in the garage. He flips the lid open and releases a combination of smells that makes my mouth water and my teeth itch: Week-old chicken wing bones. Apple cores. Paper towels used to sop up sausage grease.

Madden bends into the can at the waist, and I fear it might chomp him in half. He lifts up a white bag and squints as if he can see through the plastic. He huff-puffs again. Ever since Mrs. Shadrick asked Madden to bring back her chewed-up baton, he's been breathing like that, heavy and dramatic. Perhaps he's contracted a rare breathing disorder. I've noticed a lot of his peers breathe similarly. Perhaps it is contagious.

Madden pokes a fingernail into the plastic and slowly begins sifting through the garbage inside. He piles the garbage on the floor of the garage, moves to the next bag.

Yes! Here, I can be of great assistance. I stick my nose down deep in the garbage and my nostrils quiver—seriously, is there anything as lovely as the smell of three-day-old fish? I fling trash behind me with the might and fury of my massive paws. *Scoop. Fling. Scoop. Fling.* My claws curl around a piece of plastic wrap coated in mayonnaise. My paws squish into . . . I don't know what. Pudding?

Mixed in with all these delicious delicacies are hundreds of tiny slips of paper painted red with Madden's blood, dozens and dozens of greasy plastic tubes that smell like his salty medicine. They dot this garbage everywhere, like confetti.

"Zeus, no! Bad dog!"

I pause, look up. A glob of moldy yogurt drips off one of my left whiskers.

"Sit, Zeus!"

I sit. Upon a moist wad of toilet paper, I believe.

Madden continues to pick through the garbage, piece by heavenly-smelling piece. His lips curl; my mouth waters. His nose wrinkles; my nostrils widen. He shivers with disgust; I shiver with delight. Why is garbage so lovely?! It is a poem of smells.

He obviously needs my help. I plunge my nose into something peppery, and I sneeze, propelling a chicken skin across the room. My paws squish into the pile, and I dig furiously, scooping and flinging bits of egg-shell and ramen wrappers. A slick black banana peel sticks to the window of the lieutenant's truck. What are we looking for again? It doesn't matter: GARBAGE PARTY!

"Zeus, NO! Bad dog! Stop digging in the garbage!"

Another *bad dog*. If you're keeping score from the last few days: Bad Dog = 3, Whoossa Good Boy = 0.

And why does he get to go through the garbage, but I don't?

Madden raises the stick I chewed over his head. "Aha!"

That's what he was looking for? Why didn't he just ask me to sniff it out? I could've told him exactly where it was: lodged between the aluminum foil coated in steak fat and a few wilted stalks of old asparagus.

Madden looks at his wrist collar. "Oh! We're gonna be late meeting Ashvi!"

He shoves the stick into his back pocket. His eyes scan the scene in the garage: piles of garbage all over the floor, bits of garbage strewn about—whew! What an excellent way to decorate a room!

"I'll clean it up when we get back," he mutters. He glances at me. "I don't suppose you want to stay here?"

I blink. *I go where you go. That's the deal.*

As if he hears me, he grabs my leash and his tuba, and off we go.

★ 17 ★

COME SAY THAT TO MY BILL

Ashvi stands at the top of the hill that overlooks the pond, and I'm so happy to have her and Madden here together, in the *who wants to go outside*, heading toward those silly quacking ducks, that my back feet start walking faster than my front feet and I end up doing that thing where I walk *sideways*.

"Sorry we're late," Madden says, his voice tumbling grumbly gravel. He shifts, and I get a waft of garbage smell off him. Boy, I hope Ashvi smells that. She will be totally charmed if she knows how good he is at sifting through garbage bins. "I had to stay after school, and then I had to . . . find something."

Madden and Ashvi plop onto a wooden bench

at the top of the hill, and I sit next to Madden on the cold grass. The ducks twitch their black beady eyes my way. *YOU! YOU'RE! BACK! GO! AWAY! SHOO!*

My back legs twitch. I want to chase them so badly. But Madden hasn't unclipped my leash or vest.

Ashvi digs out a baggie full of things that look like red ropes. She tilts the bag toward Madden, and it smells like raspberry. "Can you eat red licorice?"

Madden has already plunged his hand in the bag. He chomps down on one, rips it in half. Impressive, this display of strong teeth. It is always wise to show off your assets to someone you wish to woo. Like garbage-can diving. Or peeing on things to mark them as yours.

"I can eat anything," he says around a mouthful of red goo. "I just have to correct for it."

Ashvi narrows her eyes. "So you shouldn't."

Madden grins, and he's stuck a large glob of goo to his two front teeth. I roll my eyes—what a terrible way to show your affection! Showing them what you'd look like toothless? *Defenseless?!*

"Technically," he says around the glob in his mouth, "you shouldn't eat this crap, either."

"Fair point." Ashvi laughs. And then she takes a bite of the stuff they've both agreed is *crap*, which I'm fairly certain means *excrement*, and hey, listen. I'm speaking as someone who has lapped up my own vomit here, but crap *definitely* falls into the DO NOT INGEST category.

I will never understand young humans.

YOU! DUMB! DOG! YOU'VE! GOT! FLEAS! the ducks shout across the pond, then roll all over themselves, honking at their humor. *Fleas. Ha-ha*, I grumble at them. *Like I haven't heard* that *one before, flat feet!*

COME. SAY. THAT. TO. MY. BILL!

Madden's blood is growing slowly sweeter as he eats his red rope. I perk open my nostrils to see if he needs a nudge. But he can tell his blood is shifting, because he does a quick check of his CGM. "Hey," he says to Ashvi, lowering his sleeve. "Guess my blood sugar."

Ashvi's brows pull together. "What, like O positive?"

Madden smiles. "That's a blood type. Guess a number."

"Uh . . . eight hundred sixty."

Madden bursts out a laugh like a trumpet blart. Ashvi punches him lightly on the arm and frowns, but her eyes twinkle. Humans do that all the time: their faces shift one way, but their eyes hint at something different. So confounding.

"Eight hundred sixty would be the worst blood sugar ever, probably. Guess between eighty and one-twenty."

"Okay, ninety, then."

"Close," Madden says. "I'm at eighty-eight. Zeus, you're fired. Ashvi, I'd like to offer you the position of being my continuous glucose monitor. It's a full-time gig. No nights or weekends off."

WHAT?

Fired?!

I panic. I pant.

Fired is a less-fancy human word for *reassigned*. But apparently this is more human humor, because Ashvi laughs and shoves Madden at this offer of employment.

"Hey!" she says. "Will that thing read my blood sugar?"

"No, but I could test it with a test strip."

"Let's try it!"

"Really?"

"Sure!"

I could tell them that this is a silly idea; Ashvi's blood sugar is fine. I would've told her if it weren't. But Madden fumbles with his tuba case and pulls out his black canvas test kit. He whisks it open, *zipzipzip*, and his scent changes; his smell shifts from the braggy scent of red rope licorice back to the smell of sifting through garbage. He tries to cover up the dozens of smears of blood inside the kit with his hand.

Madden removes a piece of black plastic from this

case and gently takes Ashvi's hand. He cleans one of her fingers with a wipe, something he rarely does himself. The smell burns—ammonia? The heat radiating off Madden feels like standing next to a blasting hair dryer. "Okay, so this is a little like stapling your finger."

"You know what stapling your finger feels like?" She giggles. There is a nervous undertone to her laugh, and it reminds me of tiny aphid holes eaten through the petals of a rose.

Madden leans back. "You don't have to try this."

Ashvi smiles, and suddenly it feels as if Madden and I are curled up next to a cozy fire, him in fuzzy slippers, me chewing on fuzzy slippers. "No, do it! But what if my blood is all whack—*ouch!*"

The black plastic *pops* against Ashvi's skin, and she winces.

"Sorry," Madden says softly. "It's better when you can be taken by surprise." Madden squeezes her finger gently, coaxing a small bead of blood to rise on the side of it. He swipes a test strip across it and inserts the slip of paper inside a black plastic contraption.

Ashvi leans over his shoulder and watches the screen of the monitor. Madden's internal organs melt into goo, but he still manages to sit upright. Thank goodness for skeletons. "One hundred three? Is that bad?"

It's not. You're perfect, I say.

"It's not. You're perfect," Madden echoes. Then he blazes as red as a chili pepper. "Uh . . . LY good. Perfect-*ly* good! I mean, you're fine. Yeah."

He runs a hand through his hair. *Just tell her you love her, dude.*

Ashvi's scent changes. It is full of questions, like the smell of a spring forest. "Do you think of yourself as sick? Because I don't. I don't really think of your diabetes at all."

Madden gulps, leans back. "Huh. Sometimes it feels like it's all I think about. It's definitely all my mom thinks about. But *sick*? Nah, that's not what I'd call it. More . . . inconvenient. Awfully inconvenient."

HEY. DOG. HEY! SCAREDY. DOG. YOU! YOU'RE. SCARED. LIKE. A. TINY. CHI. HUA. HUA.

The stupid laughing, honking ducks shake Madden out of his trance. "Watch this." He smiles at Ashvi, and he unclips my leash and vest.

The second that vest is off, I *spring* from my back feet and pounce-bound-bounce around the pond, chasing every last one of those fowl into the icy water with my mighty barks. Ashvi laughs but yells, "Don't eat them, Zeus!"

I sneeze sneeze sneeze because of the joy of the chase. When I'm running like this, my jowls flap in the frosty air and my back paws reach up and over my front paws and the wind tinkles my fur and I feel as unstoppable as a cold mountain waterfall.

I know I should behave better. I can *feel* my father scolding me—*Calm down, Zeus! Blend in! Be invisible like your tail!* But these ducks, this air—well, ignoring those things is as impossible as ignoring a dropped French fry.

Madden and Ashvi pop open soda bottles— "Cheers!"—and drink a slug or two each. From across the pond, I see Ashvi lay her lip against the rim of the bottle and blow—*whoooo!*

Music!

Madden does the same, but his soda music is a little higher pitched: *wheeeeeee!*

They can make music without instruments?

Ashvi laughs and says in a voice like salt on caramel, "I didn't know tuba players knew how to play like that. I thought tuba players just blew as hard as they could and hoped they made noise."

Madden laughs—*laughs!*—and instead of just a single *ting!*, his heart skips an entire little ditty, a wind chime in a storm.

They blow into their soda bottles—*wheee whooo wheee*—and their laughter interwoven with their soda music is like watching the sky stir purple and the first dots of light twinkle across the night. These two can make music without instruments. They can make music with anything! This tells me two things:

1. This mission—Operation Destroy Music—will be harder than I originally thought, and
2. Madden truly is the boy who captures stars.
6. (Bonus: I'm learning to count in the class called Number Pushing!)

★ 18 ★

THE VALEDICTORIAN (AGAIN)

Madden's feet *sliiiiiide* the whole way home. His grin looks like he's just gobbled up his fill at an all-you-can-eat trough. The sharp, clean smell of our house cuts through the air, and when we round the corner, it is mixed with the scent of—

Uh-oh.

"Madden Phillip Malone, what is all this?" The lieutenant has one fist knotted against her hip. The other hand is a terrible, poking point, directed at the piles of garbage in the garage.

Flies have started gathering around this feast, buzzing one of the two words they know: *foooooooood*. (The other is *poooooop*.) Smell rises off the garbage like a green, soupy mist. Delectable!

"I, uh, had to find something," Madden says, touching the stick still in his back pocket.

"Hmmm," the lieutenant says, her toe tapping against the cold pavement. "Well, now you're going to find the bottom of some new garbage bags, and then you're going to find a can of Lysol to clean this mess up, and *then* you're going to find your bedroom for the next two weeks, because you're grounded, son."

Madden puffs and puffs and puffs, and I fear he might *pop!* "But I was about to come clean all this up! Grounded? *Gah.* Nana and PopPop would've understood! They would've laughed and helped me clean!"

"Nana and PopPop aren't here, though, are they?"

"BECAUSE YOU TOLD THEM NOT TO COME."

The air feels icy and heavy, flash frozen in a thick, cold fog. The lieutenant works her jaw. "Did you wash your sheets this morning?"

I can *smell* Madden wanting to answer no but realizing he can't because she obviously knows the truth. "Yes."

"Why?"

"They were dirty."

"Dirty?" The lieutenant exhales a long breath, like salt pouring from a cup. "Did you have . . . an *episode*?"

Madden smells both smoky embarrassed and fiery mad. "No!" He inhales sharply. Their breathing is opposite, I notice. *Antonyms.* Tug-of-war. "You're always saying that my room smells like boy. So I washed them."

"You did laundry." It's a statement, not a question. The lieutenant's eyes narrow.

"Yes. Nana and PopPop taught me how. They also taught me how to read music and how to identify poison ivy and how to *manage my own life by my own self.*"

Madden's words are sharp, and he means them to slice. And from what I can tell, they work; the lieutenant looks hurt.

"Laundry or not, you're still grounded, Madden. Now clean this up." The lieutenant slams inside the house.

"Yes, ma'am." Madden salutes the slammed door, grabs a fistful of plastic, and begins shoving the garbage into bags.

Oh! *Oh!* He needs my help!

I sift through a pile of eggshells and find a plastic bag with a few scraggly pieces of moldy bread. I gently bite the bag and try to bring it to Madden, but I step on a tissue with a wad of gum inside. I sit—*yick!*—on the lid of a can of creamed corn. I fling fling fling my paw, but the gum is STUCK. I wriggle and scrape and dig and—

"Zeus, no! Bad dog! Stop digging! *You're* the reason I'm in trouble here. Bad dog!"

Madden's scowl makes my tail tuck. My head droop. My ears flatten.

I realize suddenly: I *am* the best at something. The valedictorian.

I am the valedictorian of being a Bad Dog.

⋆ 19 ⋆

A MASCOT!

In Number Pushing the next day, Ashvi twiddles her fingers along the length of her pencil, and I realize she's practicing playing the notes of her duet with Madden. I love her. I tell her as loudly as I can with my eyes. I can even forgive her for wearing a T-shirt with a sparkly unicorn on it. Disturbing creatures, unicorns. I hope I never encounter one.

After class, Ashvi hops up to Madden while he's slamming his Number Pushing book shut. "Hey, want to practice again today?"

Madden lights up and snuffs out as quickly as a match in the wind. "I can't. I'm grounded for two weeks."

"Two weeks? How are we supposed to practice?" Ashvi's forehead looks adorable even when it's knotted with worry. "I really want to ace this duet. I think Mrs. S might pick us to play it at state if we do a good job."

The scent of Jake materializes behind us; it's a mixture of instrument grease and zit cream. The scent of a villain. "Huh. If you can't practice the part, Malone, I'll let Mrs. S know I can take over for you."

Madden spins. His heart thrums like a drumroll, but his voice is as steady as a trumpet. "No. I got this. Ashvi, uh . . . yeah. I'll meet you at the pond again today."

Stupid *music*!

Now Madden is breaking our pack rules to find ways to play it.

Music is making Madden *outstanding*.

Music is making Madden a *rebel*.

Music is making Madden *spontaneous*.

I will find a way to quash you, music. *I will.* You will not confuse me with your spellbinding melodies.

Humans have this saying: *dogged determination*. It's fancy human words for *stubborn*. That's me. DOGged. I grumble at music, wherever it lurks: *I will defeat you, foe!*

I stand, I shake my whole self, and my tags jangle

like the sleigh bells in band.

Aha! Music has accepted my challenge.

Madden hands the stick I chewed up to Mrs. Shadrick that afternoon. He does not make eye contact with her, a submissive stance in dog-speak. But Mrs. S chuckles, and it gives Madden permission to flicker his gaze to hers.

She's flipping the baton to and fro. I did quite a number on that stick, if I do say so myself. It is dented and bent and splintery, and just looking at it now makes me want to chew it again. My mouth waters. The drool wants what it wants.

"Eh, I've seen worse," she says.

"No way." Madden laughs, and we take our seats.

Mrs. S taps the chewed baton on her podium to gather the attention of the pupils, and Madeleine Fleece's hand shoots into the air. "Mrs. Shadrick? Why is your baton all . . . ruined?"

Mrs. S looks appalled, fingertips to chest, mouth wide. "Ruined? No! Just . . . decorated. By our mascot, Zeus."

Chairs screech and instruments clang silent as all eyes turn my way. I sit taller, lift my chin higher. A mascot!

Mass. How dense an object is.

Cot. A makeshift bed.

I've never understood how calling someone a dense bed is a compliment, but I do know that being called a *mascot* is like getting a Whoossa Good Boy!

"A quick note about the upcoming holiday concert before we begin, musicians," Mrs. S says. "You must wear all black. No exceptions. If you're wearing it, it's black."

Madeleine's hand shoots into the air. Mrs. S's eyes barely flicker her way. "Yes, Madeleine. Sparkles are allowed. But only if they're black."

Madeleine's hand slides back to her lap. Mrs. S turns on the awful *tick tick tick*, which I now know is called a Dr. Beat metronome. The kids straighten their backs, lift their instruments.

"Page sixty-two, kids. 'Where the Sun Breaks Through the Mist.' One-two-ready-PLAY!"

The song features roiling drums and cymbal crashes bursting through a brassy hum and high flutes, and it sounds exactly like sunshine surging through storm clouds, just as the song's label says. The pupils banging the cymbals and drums smile every time they play over and through the other music, and I can't help but smile back at them—they're having so much fun.

"Really *hit* that drum, Jimmer!" Mrs. S shouts above the climbing notes. "POUND it! It's not going to hit you back!"

The drummer laughs and pounds the drum harder, and it's like his booming laughter spins into a booming bass line.

"There you go!" Mrs. S says, waving that chewed-up baton about. My gnawing did nothing to stop this. "All my conducting motions won't mean a thing if you don't put the emotion in!"

My nose tingles; my throat tightens. I can *hear* it. I can hear their emotions winding through tubas and trumpets and triangles. Skipping over the silver keys on a clarinet. Curling through the mellow curves of a saxophone. Sliding out of the long, slippy trombone. Flipping off the nose tips of the flute players as they lift their heads to hit the high notes.

I can hear joy!

Humans are terrible at talking about what they feel. And since they don't have tails or big tongues, they use these instruments to *show* it. For a glimmer of a moment, like the tinny triangle somehow making itself heard underneath all these other layers of music, I understand: music is emotion in sound. It is giggles and tears and sighs and wishes, and I'm here lying in a warm curl of blanket, toasted by all this joy.

DRAT YOU, MUSIC! I'M ON TO YOU! STOP WEAVING YOUR MAGIC ABOUT!

The last note ends loud, flat, fart-like, and the pupils lower their instruments and laugh. Their giggles are no longer notes hopping about. They are the red-faced breaths of kids who don't have their instruments to translate their embarrassment into music. But there is no giggly tail wag from me. Stray notes like that *hurt*. Like a punch inside my head, because my hearing is so much better than human hearing.

Mrs. S grins. "That was *great*, guys. All the way up to that last note. That one was a real stinker." The kids laugh, because if a music note could smell, that's exactly what its scent would be. "We weren't together on that last whole note. If we can nail that, we've got it."

The bell shrieks, and kids begin slamming instruments into cases.

"Wait!" Mrs. S shouts, and the kids calm. They love her and her *business*.

"The fund-raising stuff is in! We're still sorting it, but it should be ready for you to deliver to everyone who placed an order, starting tomorrow."

The pupils all groan, and boy, do I get it.

Fun. Good times, like tennis balls or Frisbees.

137

Razor. Getting groomed, which is never good times and involves scissors near *very delicate places.*

It sounds like *funrazors* means all these kids are getting groomed, right here in the band room in front of each other. Mortifying!

"I know, I know," Mrs. S says with a flip of her wrist. The trombone player takes that as a conductor's signal, and he plays a quick *whomp-whooomp.* The pupils laugh, as does Mrs. S.

"But hey, we sold enough product this year to pay for our trip to the state band competition! Our band gets to play music longer and in front of more listeners because of all those goodies."

She points the chewed-up baton toward a heap of boxes near her desk, and my eyes draw a straight line from where my teeth once were to where my teeth should go next:

Because *holy wow,* inside those boxes is FOOD, if the pictures on the front are correct! My nostrils open wide, and beneath layers of cardboard and packing plastic, I smell it: sausages and cheese and nuts and jellies and crackers and *food of all kinds*!

I blink as my brain puts all of this new information together:

If I destroy that food, the band can't go to the state competition.

If the band can't go to state, Madden has to stop playing music.

If I eat, they stop.

I WAS BORN FOR THIS MISSION.

Tomorrow, I feast.

★ 20 ★

THE THREE OF US WIN STATE

Backpack + tuba + Zeus on the bus = utterances from Madden that would put those ducks to shame. (Also: I'm learning formulas in Number Pushing!)

We *clatter-clang-bang* up the narrow bus steps. Jake and his buddies laugh; their odor is strong and teasing and taunting, like pizza when it's still too hot to eat. Madden has to maneuver his tuba in front of himself, and I follow, so neither of us sees when Jake slides his foot into the aisle just before we pass.

Madden trips. His fall is broken by his tuba case whacking into Jesus's head. Jesus leaps up, fists balled. The bus holds its breath.

His eyes land on Madden, who burns and fumbles

dozens of "Sorry, dude. Sorry. I, uh, guess I tripped." But Jesus's gaze slides toward Jake's back, his shaking shoulders. Jesus swipes at his forehead.

This situation smells sticky as peanut butter.

"No problem," Jesus says at last. "You and Zeus want to sit here? I'll hold your tuba."

Relief smells like hot laundry fresh from the dryer, and Madden practically explodes with the scent. "That'd be great. Thanks!"

We squeeze in next to Jesus, and I ball up at their feet. Jesus's left knee bounces constantly, and his scent is a big family who hug each other a lot.

"Dude, that duet with Ashvi is fierce," Jesus says, tapping the side of Madden's tuba case. "All those eighth notes? That is *tough*."

Madden nods. "Easier than those sharps you have, though."

Jesus grins, and his smile is fast and easy. "Maybe. At least you'll have some lungs left at the end of the show. After my trumpet solo on 'Ode to Joy,' I feel like I'm breathing through scuba gear."

They both laugh. I'm uncertain what scuba gear is, but it is apparently hilarious.

"That solo's going to win us state, though," Madden says after his chuckle, and he immediately looks as though he wishes he could vacuum the words right back into his mouth. But Jesus grins wider, drums a small ditty on the side of the tuba case with his fast fingertips.

"Thanks, dude. You nail that duet with Ashvi, and I bet Mrs. S will keep it in our lineup for state, too."

"Yeah?"

"Yeah. That bit is smooth."

They chat for a few more minutes about things they are passionate about called *Smash Brothers* and Doritos. When we get to Madden's stop, Jesus carries the tuba to the front of the bus, and he accidentally bonks it against the back of Jake's head as we pass.

Jesus hands the tuba case down the steps to Madden on the curb. "Me, you, and Ashvi," he says, nodding. "Nail that duet and we got this. The three of us? We can win state for Page."

The bus doors screech closed, and the yellow machine disappears in a gray cloud of exhaust.

Madden watches the bus disappear, and he chuckles like he has rocks in his throat. "The three of us, win state," he mutters, and places his fingers lightly on the tip-top of my head. "No pressure, eh, Zeus?"

And then Madden mutters something more shocking than stepping on a fire ant hill. He toes the sidewalk and says, "Win state. Huh. That'd be awesome."

He *wants* to win?

He *wants* to be outstanding?

Oh my. This mission just got that much harder.

"Sorry about the bus," the lieutenant says while getting eaten by the truck in the driveway. "I need a new alternator. This one keeps crapping out. How's your day? Insulin levels good?"

Madden shifts his weight, works his jaw. He smells guilty, but I don't know why. "I'm going to set my bags down and take Zeus for a walk, okay?"

"Roger that," she replies, which makes me wonder if Madden's middle name is Roger.

Madden walks straight through the house, drops his backpack at the foot of the stairs, and strides out the back door with his tuba case in hand. We circle through the backyard and head to the pond.

Huh. Being *grounded* doesn't mean what I thought it means. By the way the lieutenant said it yesterday, I thought it was a Bad Dog for Madden. A fence, keeping him penned in.

Ashvi is already there, and her whole self smiles and shines when she sees us.

YOU. MUTT. BACK. SO. SOON? EAT. MY. FEATHERS, the ducks taunt me from across the pond. *NICE. LEASH. LOSER.*

I wink at them. Pant. Beneath the thick glassy ice,

143

shadows of fish lurk and slide. I can *just* make out the faint winter heartbeat of the frog who has buried himself in the frosty mud near the edge of the pond, and I nudge nudge nudge it with my nose.

Ashvi and Madden sit and snack and spew orangey cracker crumbs everywhere and they take turns burning with awkwardness, which seems like an unpleasant way to pass the time. They open their instrument cases and giggle when they have to use Ashvi's flute to dig Madden's sheet music out of the horn of his tuba.

Madden unclips me at last.

I begin my haul around the pond, my paw pads instantly raw from the icy deep black mud. The ducks scream and paddle out into the water, and I laugh. *Not so brave once the leash comes off, are you, now?*

But I pull up short, because *there*, carried on a light breeze, I detect it: Madden's blood sugar is high. Too high. Lifting and getting higher, like a squeaky balloon.

I spin and chase back to the bench. Madden and Ashvi have started practicing, and their *twee*s and *toot*s bounce across the surface of the pond like those rocks Madden likes to skip. The effort of the tuba + the cold = not great for Madden.

I lick him. He pushes me away with his knee.

I nudge him. He nudges me back and laughs at a face Ashvi makes.

I circle the bench, once, twice, three times. I tickle his hand with my whiskers. Boy, do I ever wish I could bark! Ashvi offers Madden another orange cracker. He places two in his lips and quacks like those stupid ducks. *NICE. LOOK. KID*, the ducks scream. I paw his leg.

"No cracker crumbs through the tuba," Ashvi says, and Madden tosses his head back and gulps both crackers down like a pelican gulping a pair of fish.

"*So. Dry!*" He laughs and spews neon-orange crumbs everywhere.

This is serious. And I don't just mean Madden's severe lack of table manners.

Madden is *not* listening to me.

I know what I must do. Madden isn't paying attention and doesn't notice when I leave.

Left-left-right is the path back home, and I run it as fast as I can. Which is *fast*, when I'm off that short leash. The lieutenant is still in the driveway, thankfully. I lay my cold nose on her leg, and she bolts upright, her wrench clanging against the engine. *An F-flat*, I think of the sound it makes. I shake it off. Music, *now*?

Don't you get in my head, music!

She blinks at me. "Zeus? Is everything . . ."

Her eyes widen and her scent changes from motor

oil to spewing volcano. "Where's Madden, Zeus? Where is he?"

She understands!

I jerk my head in the direction of Madden's scent; poor humans and their silly little downward-facing nostrils, always smelling the ground instead of *out*. I turn and lead her back to the pond: right-right-left. Madden and Ashvi are still on the bench, and I can smell how sky-high his blood sugar is from here. He smells like lollipops, fragile like sugary glass.

"Madden Phillip Malone!"

Phillip, right. His middle name is not Roger.

Madden spins. He blinks from his mom to me, back to his mom. "Uh, hi? We were just, uh . . ."

"What's your blood sugar?" the lieutenant barks. She can be very doglike.

Madden gulps, looks at the screen on his arm. "The CGM says two hundred. But, uh, I'll double-check."

Madden bumbles his test kit out of his instrument case. While he's stapling his finger, Ashvi stands.

"Hi, Mrs. Malone," she begins.

"Lieutenant Malone," the lieutenant says.

Ashvi's skin scalds pink as salmon. "Oh! I'm sorry. It's nice to meet you, Lieutenant. I'm Ashvi Patel. I'm in band with Madden." She extends her hand.

The lieutenant eyes the hand, then grips it. "Did you know my son is a diabetic?" She tips her head to the pile of snacks between them on the bench. Madden's embarrassment smells like burnt toast, charred and dry.

"Yes, ma'am."

"Did you know my son is grounded?"

Ashvi purses her lips. She looks pained, like she's licked a lemon. "Yes, ma'am."

"I see." The lieutenant whips toward Madden. "Level?"

"Two eighty-six," Madden replies. I pace. I don't know what that number means, exactly, because Number Pushing hasn't taught me about that yet, but I know Madden is unsafe, floating in sugar. He sees white; he smells like shards of rock candy sugar.

"Did you bolus?"

"Yes, ma'am," Madden replies. "Just now. The level should come down pretty quickly . . ."

The lieutenant huffs her impatience. She turns to Ashvi. "What instrument do you play?"

Ashvi blinks like sun on snow. "The flute," she says, lamely holding her instrument up. "Madden and I were practicing our—"

"It's all good!" Madden leaps up, interrupting

147

Ashvi. "Look, mom. My CGM says one ninety-three now. Almost back to the zone." He attempts a chuckle. It sounds like the leftover flat notes played in band.

The lieutenant's arms are knotted across her chest, her lips are knotted across her face. I can smell her frustration, bitter and dark like coffee. "Get your tuba, Madden."

"Yes ma'am," he mutters. He unscrews the bell from the body and packs it away.

The lieutenant turns her knotted-up self toward Ashvi. "You seem like a nice kid, Ashvi. But you're not to see my son outside of school. Not for the next two weeks. Understand?"

Ashvi looks at the lieutenant's shoes. They are shiny, scuff-free, smooth as the ice on our pond. "Yes, ma'am. I'm sorry, ma'am."

"Me too. Thank goodness for Zeus, here." At this, the lieutenant pats me roughly on the knob of my head. It is the least pleasant patting place, this knock on my skull. I wince.

She spins and marches off. Madden picks up my vest out of the brown wintry grass and approaches me.

"Thanks a *lot*, Zeus," he mutters into my large, pointy ear as he clips my vest on. There's something about those words: just like his blood sugar, they are plummeting in sweetness. His scent says the opposite of his words. I find him *maddening* all over again.

You are welcome, I say back, and I am the opposite of him. I am earnest. I mean it. He was in danger. I'd get him in trouble with the lieutenant all over again if it means saving him.

★ 21 ★

MURDEROUS PIGS

Days later, we study a poem in Language Arts labeled "The Pig" by a fellow named Roald Dahl. Pig is smart: he can do math and he knows things like how engines work and how airplanes fly. What Pig *doesn't* know is this: Why are we all here? On Earth? What is life all about?

I nod along, listening to pig's plight. *Yes, pig! Yes! So much to learn but WHY?* But then the pig gets all murdery and he loses me. Seriously—I fear this poem might give me nightmares for weeks. But mmmm. Bacon. (That's mentioned in the poem, too. My stomach may have announced my love for cured pork products at that point.)

The rest of the classes are the same same same. But then comes band. Always new, always exciting. Always confusing, because band is the *enemy*! It cannot be enjoyable!

"We're going to practice outside on the bleachers today, kids," Mrs. Shadrick announces. "We have a pep rally next week, but we can't practice in the gym. Plus, well, it's a balmy fifty degrees out and I want to work on my tan."

The kids all laugh, then bang and clatter toward the big metal door in the back of the room that leads outside.

On the way out, many of the students sneak me a pat or a pet, and it makes me all zippy, and Madden just smiles and says nothing. "Hey, Zeus!" "Hi, Z!" "Whoossa sweet boy?" My heart is full to bursting.

There is a huge, clangy metal structure outside, and the pupils overtake it like termites. It squeaks and squeals under their weight, and I think of Mr. Dahl's murderous pig. I shudder.

"Madden, make sure that door is propped open, okay?" Mrs. S yells across the field to him. "We don't want to get locked out!"

Madden jams a rubber stopper under the door and dashes to go find his spot on the bleachers.

I blink and peer back inside the quiet classroom.

There, lined up along the far wall: the FUND-RAISERS.

This is my chance! Destroy the fund-raisers, destroy the music.

I glance back at the musicians, but they're all eyes on Mrs. S, tiptoeing into their songs. Their music sounds so different outside, like it's climbing to the clouds.

I crouch.

I flatten myself, stiffen my tail.

This gives me camouflage. I have a hard time breaking down that label, *camouflage*, but it has *moo* in it, and cows are the most polite animals you'll ever meet, so it has to be pretty good, right? Every dog has this camouflage superpower: crouch and tuck.

I *sneeeeeeak* inside.

My toenails echo on the cold, hard floor. I weave through the chairs and music stands.

I sniff the boxes—*assorted meats and cheeses*. It's the best thing about humans, really: their ability to make food like this.

I make quick work of the cardboard, rapidly chewing boxes into pulpy mulch. The plastic is not as much fun; it tastes like chemicals and oil, and it becomes overly slick from my own slobber. But I gnaw it apart bit by bit and spit it out—*patoo*—and eventually hit: YES.

Gooey yellow cheese. Mmmm, delicious fermented cow udder secretions.

Crunchy, hearty almonds. Mmmmm, earth nuts.

Fruit. I skip that.

Salty, springy sausage. Mmmmm, fat and pork pieces, and I don't feel the least bit guilty because not only am I destroying music here, but the world has one less murderous pig in it thanks to this hunk of meat. My teeth *pop* through the skin of the sausage and I chew and drool, drool and chew.

I do this again and again. Whew, these kids sure know how to fund-raise. There are boxes and boxes to go. But I can do this. I can defeat these meats and meat by-products.

My belly starts to ache, but I cannot be deterred. I am thirsty beyond belief, but I cannot be deterred. My chin drips with drool, my jaws grow tired, my tongue feels like sandpaper. I CANNOT BE DETERRED.

Suddenly, a pupil laughs right outside the door. "I just figured out how to do a thing," she says, and she blows a note into her instrument that sounds low and belly-gurgling, like a bullfrog. The door swings wide, painting the room with sunlight and cool air and the scent of grass and kid sweat.

The pupils push forward, making all the noise of a

middle school band, but they screech to a halt.

They push more.

They stop again.

"What is it?"

"What's going on?"

"It stinks in here! Is that—*oh*!"

They're all looking at me.

I smile. A glob of slobber-coated cheese drips off my jowls.

Madden works his way to the front of the crowd and stops when he sees me. His face is this math formula: embarrassment + anger.

I don't understand why he's not thanking me; they all groaned so loud every time fund-raisers were mentioned. But I go ahead and repeat what I said yesterday: *You're welcome, Madden. YOU ARE WELCOME.*

★ 22 ★

THIS WON'T DO AT ALL

"**C**an you see me?" Madden adjusts one of his blue screens, propping it against a book on his desk. Ashvi's smiling face is there. *Ashvi!* I wag, but I don't think she can see my happy tail.

"Yes!" she says. "See? FaceTime is gonna work just fine for practice. We'll nail this duet, and then Mrs. S will ask us to play it at state."

Madden cracks his knuckles under his desk, where Ashvi can't see them. *Snap snap POP!* My whiskers twitch; he's as nervous as a cat walking a fence. "It'll be great."

Ashvi is here, but she's not here, no scent of her anywhere, and I spin to try to find her in this room.

Nope, just the slightest glimpse of my tricky tail. And the other direction: nope, still my almost tail. I'm confused, so I whine. Madden doesn't notice; he's wincing as his tuba rests on his insulin pump, grunting under its weight.

As they shimmy up to their instruments, Ashvi clears her throat. "Zeus really did a number on that fund-raising stuff."

Madden stiffens, his scent tight and uncomfortable like crusty tree bark. He gulps, and I sense that he's trying to puzzle out what to say.

"I'm sure it'll be okay," Ashvi says, though her words sound thin. "The company—they'll replace it all or something, I bet. Don't you think?"

Madden warms and shifts in his chair. The cushion *flllrrrrpppp*s, a sound like passing gas. Ashvi's eyes widen on-screen, and her lips purse.

Madden stammers, "Uh, that was my chair? I promise!"

Ashvi pops open with laughter. "I thought you'd blame it on Zeus. The chair, huh?"

Madden laughs. "Definitely the chair. But, hey, I'm not above blaming a fart on my dog."

The two laugh and begin playing, and they somehow make music even though Ashvi is only hollowly here. It's bouncy, peppy music, a pop of a dozen red ladybugs on a tree, and it fills Madden's room. I'm beginning to suspect that music is bigger than I once thought. My destroying the fund-raising meats doesn't seem to have deterred it.

They twiddle and twee through the first part of their duet, and Ashvi's flute spits out an extra *flerrrrr* at the end. Her giggle hops like a cricket through the phone. Together, she and Madden both say, "That's a solo."

Madden burns so red I could cook a hot dog next to him. "Mrs. S's jokes are contagious, I guess."

Ashvi nods, and the knot of hair on top of her head bounces like a ball and I love her. "It killed me when she told Eli, 'Son, I knew you were treble.'"

Madden grins. "I like how she points to every single rest on our sheet music and shouts—"

"You're under a rest!" Ashvi and Madden yell together. They laugh like their instruments, and Madden cools a bit. "Want to try again?"

Ashvi lifts her flute. "Let's do it. This duet is going to get us noticed. I just know it."

They play.

They're good.

They spin fresh air and green grass and blue sky and

157

yellow sun and pink flowers and leaping and zoom-
ing and dashing and chasing squirrels, all out of their
instruments. They're *very* good. They *will* get noticed.

One might even label them *outstanding*.

This won't do at all.

★ 23 ★

DON'T B-FLAT

Madden tries on a number of black shirts with black pants, tucking in the shirt, leaving it untucked. He twists and turns in front of the glassy mirror picture of himself. Madden adjusts his clothes over and over again.

"All black," he says. *"If you're wearing it, it's black.* That's what Mrs. S said."

I look at the dog in the glass. That dog is wearing a bright red vest and blue collar. That dog isn't wearing all black. *You got it all wrong, Glass Zeus.* I stick out my tongue. He sticks out his tongue, too.

"Ugh, it always shows," he mutters, yanking at the hem of his shirt. He smooths his hands over his stomach, and the boxy outline of his insulin pump is there.

"Madden, let's go!" the lieutenant's voice booms and winds up the stairs.

Madden grabs his big black tuba case, and we *bolt*, as Madden says.

The holiday concert is in the school auditorium. When I escort Madden inside, Mrs. Shadrick is there waiting on us. She smiles.

"I got a present for Zeus," she says, squatting to look me in the eyes. Her joints pop faintly as she does.

A *present*? I wag. *Present = treat*. Everyone knows that formula. I drool.

"Really?" Madden says. He looks over his shoulder to see how close the lieutenant is standing. She's chatting with another mother several paces away. He lowers his voice. "He hasn't exactly been an ideal classmate."

Mrs. S takes out a tiny black slip of material and fastens it around my neck, over my collar. Her hands are gentle and quick. It's not a treat. I try to hide my disappointment.

"He's not a classmate. He's a dog. He was just doing dog things. I should've known better than to leave boxes of food on the floor with a dog around!"

Mrs. S straightens the material around my neck. "There!"

Ashvi pops up over Madden's shoulder like a chir-rupy grasshopper. "A bow tie! So cute!" She smiles lightning bolts. I smile and sit taller, chin lifted. Okay, maybe this present isn't so bad if I get Ashvi-smiles.

Ashvi nudges Madden's shoulder with her own, and Madden smells suddenly joyous, like the *whoosh* of a new can of tennis balls popping open. "You nervous?" she asks.

"Not really," Madden says, which is the opposite of the sweat I smell on his palms, the squeak of his grit-ting teeth. Maddening. "You?"

"Gosh, yes!" Ashvi is telling the truth. Her heart races like a rabbit, and her toes drum inside her black combat boots.

"You two will be great," Mrs. S says. "Just don't *B-flat*. Get it? B-flat? A little band humor there, kids."

Ashvi and Madden grin and slide their eyes at each other.

"Go find your places, okay?"

I guide Madden to his chair, the one on the end of the row on the far right side of the stage. Jake is already in his seat, and he glares at us.

"Hey, Jake," Madden gargles in a whisper. His throat is filled with sand.

"You're only in that first chair because of your dumb *dog*," Jake whispers back, teeth gritted, barely moving his lips. "Not because of your talent. You're going to mess up that duet so hard."

Madden's heart drumrolls, and his sweetness plunges. His scent is suddenly sour yogurt. He is not in the dangerous zone, but he could be, quickly. I perk my nostrils.

The auditorium is *chaos*. I think of those dizzying balloons, lifting and spinning. So disorderly! So unpredictable!

This chaos puts me on high alert. Kids pinging and spinning off one another, cases clanging, locks clicking, instruments flashing. Nervous whispers and giggles, all crisscrossing like silvery spiderwebs. And under *that*, Madden's heart, his sweat, his sugar. I have to really focus to find it.

Eventually, everyone is in their seats, like coals cooling.

Except it's not cool at all. Up here on the stage, the lights are so bright, all I can see is hot white beams and the darkness behind them. The light pings off the brassy instruments in tiny starbursts and my eyes water. The auditorium smells of stage fright and expectancy and nervous, proud parents. All of these distractions make it harder to do my job. I strain to find Madden's scent.

Mrs. S taps on the podium with her chewed-up stick (*stick!*), and the room silences. Wow, her power!

"Ladies and gentlemen, welcome to the Page Middle School holiday band concert!"

The audience wags tails of applause.

"We've worked really hard on the selection of music you'll hear today. I think you'll love what we've put together. But I did want to let you know: if you ordered something through our fall fund-raiser, you'll need to please see me after the show for a full refund of your purchase. We had a little . . . *incident* with our fund-raising. And because of it, Page Middle won't be able to attend the state band competition this year."

What?

I did it!

I stopped the music!

The audience groans and whispers and shuffles in their seats. Sixty-some-odd band members rumble. The smell up here onstage shifts from nerves to nastiness, as though the wind were suddenly blowing campfire smoke directly into my eyes. It burns, all these gazes narrowed at me.

Next to Madden, Jake stiffens. His eyes are knives.

I can even feel Jesus—kind, funny Jesus, *Hey, Zeus!*—clench his teeth in my direction.

But worst of all: Ashvi won't even look over at us.

The most difficult missions don't earn you any friends, I'm learning. And it's been hard destroying music, but I've done it! Their season will end short because of me. Perhaps we will all just go home now.

But Mrs. S taps her stick on her podium again, and the shuffling and whispers from the audience and band settle like dust. "It's disappointing, I know. Especially for our eighth graders. But it doesn't change how hard they've worked, or how much they've grown musically. It doesn't change how much heart and joy these kids pour into their music. So sit back, relax, and enjoy the show."

At that, the lights shimmer and shift, darkening slightly. A drumroll rumbles from the opposite corner of the stage, growing slowly louder, as blurry and lovely as hummingbird wings. A cymbal crashes. My eyes grow instantly misty. My throat swells.

The kids roll almost flawlessly through the music they stumbled and tripped over in class: "Jingle Bells" and "Sleigh Ride" and "Feliz Navidad." I sit next to Madden, rather than lie, because it feels right, more distinguished, and chills race under my fur as the songs swell and swirl around me.

The xylophone tiptoes across the stage. The saxophone sneaks. The triangle hops like a frog. The drums jumble and roll, like the rhythm of tags jangling on a run. Notes float in the air, sliding over and through those beams of light, like bumblebees fat and lazy, buzzing from flower to flower.

Jesus stands and plays his trumpet solo. It is brassy yellow owl eyes swirling through midnight skies. The band slowly weaves the rest of the sound around his, lifting his music ever higher.

I hear it, I *taste* it: the joy and smiles and wonder of these musicians. The music is so powerful, I feel stinging in my nose, my eyes. I want to sneeze sneeze sneeze with joy like I do while chasing those confounded ducks, but I remember Mrs. S saying *absolutely no sneezing*. As much as I want to destroy music, I love Mrs. S and I will obey her commands.

Then Madden and Ashvi stand. Madden's heart rolls, but his scent is earthy and solid. He is confident. His tuba cartwheels and spins around Ashvi's flittering flute. Their instruments play together like puppies, one big and goofy with oversized paws, one small and yippy with sharp teeth and a quick pink smile.

Madden's tuba rumbles my core. A tingle starts in my paw pads and climbs up over my belly. Chills make my fur stand on end. I can't explain it; I can't label it. The rush of the music rolls over me and wraps me up so tightly that this stinging has to go somewhere, and I find it grumbling across my vocal cords. I made myself visible when I chased those silly bubbles; I cannot do that again! The music wants to escape me like a puppy jolting through a swung-open gate.

I cannot let that happen! I MUST remain invisible.

I whimper.

I whine.

I shift on my tailbone.

I shake. My tags jangle. *This won't do!*

Madden's gaze slides down toward me. He glares, his eyes sharp as a high C note. His frown pushes through his tuba and barks at me, putting me in my place.

Maybe if I just . . . *leave* . . . then I won't be tempted by all this confusing emotion.

I can slink offstage. Hide in the dark, cool back area. I can camouflage myself by crouching low, tucking my tail, hunching my back. All dogs have this superpower, after all. I turn to sneak into the backstage shadows. One step, two steps, three . . .

Then my collar *yanks* my neck—*hork!* I *pull*. Tug.

My leash is tangled around something. I put my whole body into it, and I *heave*!

Behind me, Madden's music stand topples with a *CRASH*!

And his music stand topples into Jake's, which topples into Gracelyn's, which topples into Kate's. The four metal stands *clattercrash boom bang clank*! Sheet music flutters up and around the tuba section like an explosion of feathers.

I run to the dark, cool backstage, dragging Madden's music stand behind me: *CLANG CLANK CRASH!* I duck behind the thick velvet curtain, peer out at the bright stage with a shiver.

The percussion section sees the issue and tries to cover my mistake. They boom the bass drum out of turn, run a mallet across the chimes, and crash the cymbals, as if it were all a part of the song. I once heard Mrs. S call this type of music *improv*. It's a fancy human word for *make it up as you go*. But it also sounds like *improve*, and it *improves* this piece. It's jazz! Many of these musicians are in the jazz band, so they apparently know how to play like this, like it's a spontaneous conversation between instruments.

It is chaos. *Jazz* is chaos—patterns woven inside the chaotic.

And? Madden glances down the row at his fellow tuba players, nods at them: *keep going*. He is their leader, their *first chair*, and they listen. They shuffle in their seats, kick the music stands gently aside, and *keep making music*.

It's not what this song is supposed to sound like. The song is supposed to sound like kittens tiptoeing and tumbling on tiny pink toe-bean feet. It now sounds like a herd of cattle escaping an avalanche. Powerful and earthy.

And the kids? They never stop playing. The drummer and xylophone player now pick up the tempo, and they trot their sound in next to the original song, adding a new layer of sound where one wasn't before. Jesus throws in an extra-powerful punch of a note, then two, then a whole little shimmy-shake with his trumpet. They make my mistake a part of their music. I didn't know music could do that: spin noise into something so lovely.

Can chaos be lovely? Surely not!

The song winds down, and the air stops its brassy shimmering.

Quiet.

The whole auditorium, every musician, every audience member, looks at me, hiding between the folds of the theater curtain. The lights get sweatier. I feel dizzy. My left ear twitches.

The room explodes with applause. Laughter.

The musicians stand. Bow. The audience stands, too.

I sneak back onstage, still dragging Madden's music stand.

The audience wags like mad, their applause loud and constant. I smell salty tears. I taste smiles. I hear snippets of whispers in the audience: "That sounded like true jazz!" and "Was that planned?" and "Those kids really know how to improvise!"

We're all standing and wagging as the music notes melt from the air around us. The whole room smells confusing and overwhelming, like tuna casserole.

I love tuna casserole.

★ 24 ★

THE EXPECTATION OF POP!

The next day is a no-school day, which usually means Madden and I sleep until the sun is high in the sky and our breath stinks of too much morning. But today, the lieutenant wakes us early and we pile into the car, voices and tummies grumbling.

We go through this thing labeled a "drive-through," which is a glorious place where they shove food through the window of your car. We get biscuits and coffee. Well, *they* get biscuits and coffee, a steamy drink that looks and smells like mud but makes hearts hummier. The lieutenant is strict about me not eating "people food," which I think is a cruel and limiting way to label 80 percent of tasty edible things. But I lap up biscuit crumbs off the floor.

Then we get on a highway. The sun is just barely peeking over the hilltops, and the grass melts from frosty white to crystal wet, and the pink sunlight glistens through the dew like tiny drops of wet fire. The tires purr on the road, and Madden's pulse purrs with them.

"You didn't tell me you had a solo in the concert," the lieutenant says, and just like that, his purrs become growls.

"A duet, actually," Madden mumbles.

"Okay, a duet. Why didn't you tell me?"

Madden lifts a shoulder, lets it drop. If we were in band, that gesture would sound like a misplaced note. I can practically hear the words inside his head: *You wouldn't listen anyway, because all you do is worry about me.* Also, *You wouldn't let me because you'd think it was too strenuous.* Also, *You didn't invite Nana and PopPop to come.* I don't know how I can hear him so clearly. How can I hear him and not be able to label him?

A silence fills the car. I mean, *fills* it. In science class recently, Madden's teacher Ms. Yang used another balloon to demonstrate a concept—*gas expansion* or

171

something like that. She exhaled into the balloon over and over again, and it slowly, gently swelled. (Humans can do *amazing* things with their breath.) The balloon filled and grew, grew and filled, and its skin became glowy and transparent. She kept blowing into that plastic pouch, and it burst with a *POP!* She blew up a second balloon then, and the expectation of that *pop* made my every strand of fur stand on end.

The silence now fills the car like that.

"You were good. You and Ashvi—you were very good."

Madden becomes glowy and transparent, too, and his scent lightens sweet and mild, like dewy drops of wet fire. He tugs on his T-shirt (which he always does when he smells embarrassed). His shirt looks like a night sky, a universe swirled with purply blue-pink clusters of stars. Chaos.

"I'm sorry you don't get to go to state," she says. "I bet you and Ashvi would kill it with that much more practice."

I know Madden is mad at me for stopping his outstanding music. And here is where he could tell the lieutenant that it's all because of me that he and Ashvi don't get to play in the big competition. He inhales, but the words *Zeus's fault* never pop out.

I don't know why.

I can't label this mix of feelings. I'm proud I'm keeping Madden from being outstanding. I am. We are supposed to be invisible, he and I. But him being mad at me is as itchy-uncomfortable as a mosquito bite.

And? I will miss music. I admit, I will miss that beguiling mystery. Now that we're not headed to "state," surely the band will just give up on making music and do other, more practical human things, like cooking meat and throwing balls and opening doors.

It is chaos. All of it.

We ride along in silence for a while longer, until the lieutenant takes a sudden left turn.

"Almost to the prison," she says. Madden nods.

The prison?

DAVE!

But, oh, the *prison*?

That means today?

Today is the day of my four-week evaluation.

Today is the day when I find out if I've been a Good Boy, and I get to stay with Madden, or if I get *re-assigned*.

I ate the sheet music. I ate the stick. I ate the fund-raiser. I ruined the concert.

There is *no way* Madden is going to keep me after

all that. So even though I'm nailing my mission, the others are going to see this as a failure. I am definitely going to be reassigned.

I hang my head, preparing to face Dave.

This swollen balloon? It's about to POP.

★ 25 ★

LEAVES OR STARS?

My heart yanks me forward into the prison, and my tail is so excited to wag at Dave it pulls me sideways. *Calm down!* I tell my tail, but it doesn't listen. It never listens. Tails don't have ears. You can't change a tail.

We don't go behind the bars this time, into the cells. Instead, we go to a room Dave rarely went when I was his roommate: the guest visiting room.

The prison smells the same: sweat and food and tiredness. Dave's scent is there, far away but approaching. I picture his footsteps echoing on the concrete floors as he nears us. Lots of things echo in a prison. Footsteps. Voices. Memories.

The door swings wide, and THERE HE IS! *I LOVE YOU, DAVE!* I forget my vest rules, and I whine and I wriggle and I hop on my two back legs and I lick his face with my wide pink tongue, *sccch-llluuurrrppp!* He tastes the same: wise with a hint of salty sadness. *Authentic.* Dave laughs but holds his hand out, palm cupped. The *sit* gesture. My butt drops to the cold, hard floor. He flips his palm over, flat. *Lie down.* I do.

Dave scratches me behind my ears, and it feels so good I close my eyes and pant. *Dave.*

Dave shakes the lieutenant's hand, then Madden's hand. Then he turns to me. "Shake, Zeus."

I sit up and offer my paw like the dignified gentleman I am. Dave laughs and shakes it. Madden smells like a pop of surprise, a smoky firecracker.

"I didn't know he could do that!"

Dave hands Madden the stack of papers he's holding. "Yeah. I forgot to give you this. It's the rest of the commands Zeus knows."

Madden flips through the many pages, a sound like wings. "Wow! Look at this, Mom. He knows all these commands? He can turn lights on and off?"

Dave nods. "When we're first training the dogs, we're not sure where they'll be a good fit. All the dogs learn those things in case they excel at assisting someone in a wheelchair."

Madden looks at me, his face shifting like he's working on a puzzle. "Dude. He's smart!"

I smile at him. *They don't call me a single, accurate bloodhound who prefers the status quo for nothing!*

The humans settle into chairs, and I try to choose who I sit beside: Dave or Madden. Dave or Madden? I decide it's easiest if I sit between them.

"So, how's it going?" Dave asks. I can't figure his voice out. He doesn't want me to be *reassigned*, does he? I think of a bit of kibble, plopping into my water bowl. At first it's great, because hey, soft meaty kibble! But the longer the kibble stays there, soaking, the mushier the kibble gets. The murkier the water grows.

This conversation feels like that. Mushy. Murky.

"It's good, I guess," Madden says. The lieutenant shifts, like this is the first time she's heard the *I guess* part. And she understands reassignments. She understands the *re* part of that word means *again*, means *backward*. Like *retreat*. Like *revert*. *Reassign*.

Dave's jaw tightens. This is it. This is where I get placed somewhere else. I clench my teeth. "Is he detecting your blood sugar levels accurately?"

Madden's mood sweetens, a puff of cotton candy.

"Oh yeah! He's really good at that."

Dave sits back in his chair, knots his fingers. "Good. He's an excellent scent dog. We trained with those scent tins for months."

Dave goes on to tell the lieutenant and Madden how they trained me: using cotton balls that people with diabetes wore in their socks. I'd smell the sweat, learn the difference between blood sugar highs and lows. It all seems straightforward to me, but Madden looks at me like I'm some sort of superhero. Like I should wear tights and a cape.

"But is there . . . something else?" Dave asks.

This is it. This is where Madden tells Dave about all the times I've been a Bad Dog. (If only I could let Dave know *why*, about Operation Destroy Music, he'd understand. I know he would.) Here comes my *re-assignment*.

"Well, he's . . . not very *obedient*," Madden says, looking at his hands. His fingers are twitching, and I can practically smell how much he wishes he could wrap himself in the safety of his tuba right now.

"Oh, service dogs like Zeus shouldn't be obedient," Dave says. He smells as confident as soap; he knows dogs. "They need to be smart. Stubborn. Wisely disobedient, in fact. He needs to pay attention to your blood sugar, and he needs to get you to do the same, no matter what it takes. That's his job."

Madden nods at the tips of his sneakers.

"Is he behaving?" Dave asks. "A *polite* dog is what we want, not an obedient dog."

"Yes, he's—" the lieutenant begins.

"No." Madden interrupts. They glance at each other. Mushy. Murky.

Dave's gaze pings between the two of them like a bouncing rubber ball. "Is Zeus . . . a good fit?"

If the silence before, in the car on the way here, was a party balloon? THIS silence is one of those huge hissing balloons that float high in the sky, ready to crash with the shifting winds.

I'm so frustrated at not having the right label for this moment. It occurs to me that a swirl of music, a mix of sorrowful sax and high-stepping clarinet, would be better at capturing how I feel right now. And that frustrates me even more. Stupid *music*!

"He's great at alerting me to changes in my blood sugar," Madden says. "But why does he keep acting out?"

Dave's voice is gentle like a cool, shallow puddle. "Are you walking him every day? Grooming him? Playing with him? A German shepherd like Zeus has a lot of energy, Madden. If you don't do those things, he'll channel his energy elsewhere."

Madden is silent. Even his pulse quiets. "I could do more of that, I guess."

"If you do, he'll be a great dog. I promise."

I will! I will be a great dog if you do those things, Madden! I'll do my very best! I thump my tail, because humans can't resist that.

But then. THEN Dave does something I never expected. He sighs, and it's filled with a mixture of scents: doubt and hope. I used to think those two labels were opposites, *doubt* and *hope*, so they couldn't possibly exist at the same time. But I'm finding that doubt and hope often walk side by side for humans.

"I tell you what," Dave says. "I don't usually do this, but let's have another evaluation in four more weeks. If Zeus is still acting out then, well . . . we'll figure something else out."

WHAT?

My stomach feels like I gulped a handful of gravel, and I have to lie down. I could still get reassigned? I can't think of anything more unfair! Or humiliating—what will my dad say once he finds out? Or the others at Canine College? Beef? Service dogs are huge gossips; they'll *all* find out once the dogs in here start flapping their tongues.

And this, coming from *Dave*! Unfair smells like turkey bacon. I huff. I turn my back on him. I huff again. I clench my jaw.

Dave and the lieutenant chat about some other things, fill out paperwork. Madden gets down on his hands and knees, looks at me.

"I'll do better if you do better, okay, Z?"

Deal. But listen. This whole thing reeks like cat pee. I won't get any more bad dogs. I will always be whoossa good boy.

Madden nods like he understands. "Shake, Z."

I offer my paw. We shake on it. It is now a *pact*, a word that sounds a lot like *pack*, so it's weighty and important. Madden's scent changes; he now smells like hope, like a fluff of musky dandelion just before its seeds fly on the wind. But there it is: a bit of doubt walking alongside it. Doubt and hope, together again.

Moments later, Madden gathers my leash. Dave stoops and hugs my neck. His heart is slow and steady and asks for forgiveness, as always. I'm sad and angry, but I have a job to finish.

Madden pauses just before we walk past the guard out the door. "Do you really think this'll work out, Mr. Dave?"

Dave grins and replies in a way that is very Dave; he points to Madden's star-spattered shirt and says:

"Which are there more of: stars in the universe or leaves on the trees?"

Madden blinks. "Uh, stars, I guess."

"But how do you know? You can see more leaves than stars."

Madden inhales, his brain ticking like drumsticks counting off a measure before a song. "I don't know. I believe what the experts tell me, I guess."

"Exactly. And I'm an expert in Zeus. I'm telling you, he's a great dog. But I'll see you in four more weeks to make sure. One month."

Madden looks at me. My ears pivot toward him.

Dave blinks. Is he holding back tears? Why doesn't he believe in me yet? Why do I have to worry about *reassignment* still hanging over my head? Why aren't there better words, better commands to tell me what to do in situations like this? I am the best at following commands. The very best. The single-accurate-bloodhound-who-prefers-the-status-quo best.

I am not so good when there are no commands to follow.

But Dave grins. "In dog we trust."

Maddens nods. "In dog we trust."

But apparently not.

Apparently, some words mean nothing.

★ 26 ★

THE SAME

In the car on the way home, a song tinkles through the radio. Madden leaps toward a button, turns up the noise.

"Stevie!" he shouts. "I love this song!"

The lieutenant's face breaks. Stretches. Into . . . *no*. A smile?

"Me too!"

The two of them howl along to the words in the song: *Signed, sealed, delivered, I'm yours!*

Madden's fingers thrum along the seam of his jeans, and I can see he's picking out the notes he'd play on his tuba, if he were playing this tune.

They are singing the same song, the same words, at

the same time. It is the first time I have seen them be the same.

They can be *the same*?

It's as sweet as the earth after a fast, hot rain on a summer day. I want this moment to last, because *the same* is the status quo, and it's what I prefer. *The same* is as comfortable as a crunchy old chew toy that tastes like months of mouth. So I regret when I smell it: Madden's blood turns, and his scent is suddenly overly salty. Low, dark, and hollow. A curl of sea.

I stand on the back seat.

I nudge him.

He laughs and scratches me behind the ear. It feels delicious, but he needs to be alerted.

I ram my head into his shoulder. Paw at him. Lick his face.

"Mom," Madden says at last. "Can you pull over? I think Zeus is telling me I need to test."

The lieutenant veers the car to the side of the road, a little too sharply. We swerve in the gravel, and I lose my footing. I tumble onto the floor of the back seat.

The lieutenant's heart is suddenly cloudy and thunderous. "The doctor said that the motion of a car can mask a low blood sugar. I should've told you to test before we left. I should've . . ." Her voice trails off like a scent on the wind.

While Madden tests, I pace the back seat, window to window. *Too low. Too low.* A low of deep ocean washing over Madden, a dot of sunlight gurgling further away. Out of one window, cars whiz past in roars of color. Out of the other, a goat lifts her head, looks our way, and bellows, *My graaaaaaaass. Get your own paaaaaaaaasture!*

Madden blinks at the number on his monitor. "Wow, fifty-two!" He digs into the drawstring backpack at his feet and gobbles down a handful of gummy bears. His face twists as he gulps them down drily— he's not hungry, but he must eat.

The sugar in his blood climbs out of the sea and washes onto the beach. The lieutenant thanks me by scratching my neck. Or trying—her fingernails are still a short, scraggly mess. Ineffective as tools of any sort. Which is always surprising to me.

Perhaps it is something that happened to her when she was reassigned, these short fingernails. It certainly seems a punishment of some sort.

The goat takes great offense to the fact that we haven't heeded her warnings. *I saaaaid LEEEAVE!*

Her eyes spin in their sockets, and she charges at us. The goat rams her head into the wooden fence next to our car. It *crack*s like thunder, making both Madden and the lieutenant jump.

185

I bark at her, *Come on! The kid's gotta eat!*

Madden and the lieutenant chuckle. I made them chuckle! I shouldn't bark in my vest, but I made them *so happy*. And, well, I'm not barking to alert anyone. It's a silly *goat*, for heaven's sake. So I bark at the confounded animal. The lieutenant smiles and swerves back onto the highway in a cloud of gravelly dust, until I can't see that stupid goat anymore.

That's riiight! LEEEEEEEEAAAAVE! the goat bellows after us.

The car is quiet, no more Stevie songs sewing Madden and his mom together, making them the same. But Madden tries something, a small stitch to get that moment back. "We're working on 'Superstitious' in band, you know. The part I play goes, *hmm frmm hmm frmm . . .*"

"Do you want to try a new insulin? Your doctor said that Fiasp is supposed to be faster-acting. And listen, before I forget, we still need to discuss that JDRF walk next month . . ."

Madden falls silent. So does the lieutenant. Silence is a big, important thing with humans, and it says more than words, usually. The lieutenant's scent changes back to the whiff she usually wears around Madden: eggshells. Cool. Chalky. Fragile.

The tires buzz.

Madden stares out his window, forehead against glass. The lieutenant looks in the rearview mirror. The windows are all foggy, so I don't know what they're looking at. I do know what they're *not* looking at. But here's what they don't know:

Their hearts are humming the same tune.

Their hearts both hum: *I want you to hear me.*

★ 27 ★

GROOMING HABITS

*S*uperstitious.

Super. To excel at something; to be a Very Good Dog.

Stitious. Well, honestly, I'm not really sure what this means, but if I'm super at it, that's all that matters.

The song we're listening to in Madden's room is the one he practices now in band. This version sings about being *very superstitious*. It also sings about *the writing on the wall*, which I assume means a whiteboard like the one they use in my school, so I know this song is about being smart and scholarly and making wise, informed choices.

Madden runs a wiry brush through my coat over and over again, and it feels so good to get all that loose hair out of my fur, my haunches shiver. He laughs and cleans the brush. "Dude. Another baby Zeus could be made with all this fur."

Well. It is certainly time for the lieutenant to discuss certain *things* with Madden, because that's *not* how babies are made.

Madden hums along to the music that shimmies out of a box on his desk, and I think what an astounding thing humming is: not singing, not silence . . . just another amazingly breathy way humans make music. It calms their hot blood, humming.

Madden cuts my toenails (*not too close, there, bub*) and trims the fur between my paw pads. He gives each paw pad a tiny massage, and it feels so good I flop over on my back and drool. Madden scratches my belly. My back left leg laughs.

He washes the gross brown gunk out of the corners of my eyes, and they are blinky clean again (*ahhhh*). He cleans my ears with a cool cleansing pad (*yessss*). He folds open my flappy lips and scrubs my teeth with a cloth. Then he hands me a green bone, and my breath feels tingly and sparkly as I wrap my paws around it and chew.

I feel like a new dog. I look for the dog that lives in the shiny glass, expecting to stick my tongue out at that ratty old fella, but would you look at that? Someone's gone and groomed that rascal Glass Zeus, too! *Hmmpf.* Show-off.

Next, Madden grooms his instrument. He flips open the locks on the black suitcase, *click click*, and pulls out the shiny brass bell of his tuba. He handles it so gently, Beef the tuba, and I feel jealousy bite me like my new tingly teeth.

Madden polishes the brass with a cloth, and the instrument brags with shine. There is a Zeus in there, too—in the gleam of the instrument, all pointy ears and lush whiskers—and *that* Zeus, Music Zeus, I like least of all.

Madden drops earthy, musky oil onto the up-down buttons of his tuba named Beef, and then smears wax inside each piece of the instrument, on the cork. He smiles. "Zeus, Ashvi's pretty great, isn't she?"

Yes. We both love her.

Madden twists his instrument to and fro, sending splashes of yellow light onto his walls. "Yeah, she's great. But she was just hanging out with us because of the duet. I know it. You watch: now that the duet is over, she'll ditch us like dirty Kleenex."

Dirty Kleenex is delicious, and speak for yourself. She loves me.

A new song wiggles out of the radio, one that sounds like chasing and leaping at playful crumples of moths. "Yes!" Madden leans forward, turns up the volume. His toes tap, his shoulders sway, his heart dances.

I can't help it: my tail wags in time with the music.

Drat! How does music get the best of me every time?

I cock my head left, then right. I don't *get it*. Music can't be contained, can't be defined with words. It is impossible to label. It has no obvious survival value; if anything, it lets defenses crumble.

Take the musicians in our band class: The red faces. The blown-out cheeks. The popping eyes. Their knees shake to hold a note. Their foreheads bulge; their necks strain. They sweat. They spit. They fart. And Madden especially: music makes his blood go wild. They do all this to create music, something so very . . . *impractical*!

Music is nonsensical.

So why does it make me feel so happy?

Madden turns all this grooming energy onto himself next. He peels off the stickers he wears on his arm and on his belly. He winces a bit as they come off. I can't say I blame him—I can hear his fur getting ripped out by the root from here.

Madden takes a white cloth that burns my nostrils with its strong chemicals and swipes it over his skin. He takes a piece of plastic and, *click click*—a sound just like the instrument case—he places a new pod in his arm. He staples another piece of plastic into his belly. More plastic is latched onto these ports.

Madden next stabs a long needle into a clear, gooey medicine and fills up the tube connected to it. I'm not going to pretend to be brave here; needles make me swoony. I can tell by the salty smell of the medicine that this is the stuff that fights his sugar. This is the medicine that helps him when he's spiraling up up up into the too-high crystal sugary whiteness. Using clear vials and plastic tubes and tiny needles and a pinch of his skin, he connects everything, and his devices beep with satisfaction.

Madden flinches as the new medicine streams into his blood through this new port. I can smell how it stings him: tiny sweat bees nibbling beneath his skin. But the whole time he's done this, the *whole time*, he hasn't stopped dancing. He hasn't stopped humming. He hasn't stopped singing under his breath, "Don't you worry 'bout a thing, mama . . ."

Madden is a fighter. He's surviving even when his body is battling him. Does music help him fight?

Humans don't always see it, but their bodies can only do so much. But their *souls*? That part of humans that makes music? Souls are unlimited.

How in the whole world of green grass am I supposed to defeat *that*?

★ 28 ★

CHASING MY TAIL

Before band the next day, Madden takes me outside for a much-needed restroom break. It's raining. A cold, hard, pelting rain. Madden shivers beneath the hood of his windbreaker. I can smell his impatience through the downpour.

We duck back inside. I can't help it: a shiver starts at the very top of my tail. I arch my back, stand on tiptoe, and *shakeshakeshake* as hard as I can to dry off. *Ahhhh.*

"No!" Madden hisses. "No shake, Zeus!"

But it's too late. Once I've started shaking, I can't just *stop*. The shake winds its way across my spine forward to my nose, then kicks into reverse and shimmies back toward my tail.

Much better.

Except now I not only have Madden's eyes poking at me, I have a new gaze jab-jab-jabbing me. This fellow leans against a mop in a bucket.

Madden gulps. His skin is practically steaming, between the rain and his embarrassment. He turns to the fellow with the mop.

"I'm so sorry, Mr. Jensen. I'll help clean that up."

But the guy is already churning the mop inside the bucket on wheels, *shhurrp shhollpp*. "No worries, kid. I'll get it." He grins. "You can't put me out of a job that easy."

A smile twitches Madden's face. "You sure? It's . . ." He looks around. "A lot of fur, too."

I smile. I am able to produce copious amounts of fur.

The fellow laughs. "It is. But, hey, I got it. You go make music. I like listening to you guys. I'm always on the band hall for the 2:10 class."

Madden's smile makes this whole wet corner glow. "Thanks, sir!"

But his smile cracks, crumbles when we walk into the band room. It's the first time we've been back since the holiday concert. Since the announcement that Page Middle is not going to the state band competition.

The mood in the room stinks like a hot sewer. The pupils fall silent when we enter; the shuffling *toot*s and *tweet*s that pop from each instrument fall flat like a stale, underthrown tennis ball. As Madden crosses the room, the xylophone player quietly taps out a song with his fingertips: *dun dun dun, dun DA dun, dun DA dunnnnn.*

I recognize the music from the first day of band, and from movie night at the prison. It's played every time that terrifying dude in the black mask swooshes into the room in *Star Wars.*

Kids giggle and titter. Madden's teeth squeak, he's clenching his jaw so tightly as we take our seats. Ashvi wads up a sheet of paper and tosses it at the xylophone kid. "Hey!" he mutters as it bounces off his noggin.

Mrs. Shadrick rushes into the room and pretends she doesn't see or hear any of this. She makes her way to the podium at the front, and the quiet is thick and tangled like matted fur.

She breathes deep. She smiles. She looks like a rosebud, ready to burst open in bloom.

"Kids!" she says, her voice trembling. "We're going to state after all!"

The next few moments are so uniquely human: the words hang in the air like laundry on a clothesline, flapping. Then the room *explodes*—chairs scraping, music stands toppling and crashing, hands clapping, kids shouting, instruments banging and tweedling.

Jesus shoots a hand in the air. "But, Mrs. S—*how*?"

Mrs. S chuckles like she can't believe it herself. "An anonymous donor was in the audience at the holiday concert. This person was so charmed by our grand finale"—here, she stops and looks directly at me, curled up on my flannel blanket. My heart speeds—"and especially with Zeus leading our impromptu jazz session, they wanted to make certain we had the chance to share that at the next level. This person is paying for us *all to go to state*!"

Sixty-some-odd kids turn to me. They hug me with their eyes.

"Atta boy, Zeus!"

"The comeback kid!"

"Nice job, boy! Way to turn it around."

Madden scritches my neck and smiles smiles smiles.

He is happy with me at last!

I stand.

I pant.

I wag.

But—*oh!*

I scan all the happy faces behind their shining, gleaming instruments.

This means more music.

This means more *outstanding*.

I am not invisible in the least. And Madden won't be, either.

Well, I'll be muzzled. I had conquered music. And then music conquered me. My toppling of those music stands brought music back.

I am chasing my tail here, it seems.

"What're we waiting for?" Mrs. Shadrick says. "We've got a state competition to win!" The kids rise, then settle, like fur fluffing off a dog bed.

The ticktock metronome clicks on. "One-two-ready-GO!" Mrs. S says, and the kids begin playing a tune that feels like a swirling stormy nighttime sky, with razor-sharp stars and a sickle moon.

A drummer hefts her puffy-soft mallet over her head, booms down on the drum that's as big as a water barrel. The night sky rumbles, stars moving like thunder. The drummer winces; it takes a lot of muscle to make a sound that big.

"Good!" Mrs. S shouts at her. "Way to show that drum who's boss, Jamie!"

The cymbals toss in a streak of lightning, white

paint thrown across the dark canvas.

The musicians spin and whirl a few more crashing banging bars, and Mrs. S quiets them. She points her chewed-up stick (*stick!*) at the triangle player. "Alan, I appreciate the fact that you played that triangle loud and proud, but you're two measures out. Check your sheet, yeah?"

The triangle pupil nods. Several members of the woodwinds bounce reeds between their lips. They look like ducks. *Confounded ducks!*

"And tubas," she says, wheeling toward us. Madden and me and Jake and the others. "Do me a favor. Play A-flat at ninety-one."

Jake's hand shoots into the air. Mrs. S shows us her palm. "I know it's wrong. Just play it."

Jake, Madden, and the other tubas play an A-flat. It sounds low and sad, tummy-rumbly, like a sugar low.

A sugar low.

I sit.

My nostrils perk.

"See how bad?" Mrs. S laughs. "Sounds like an elephant sitting on a piano." The class laughs. Madden blinks. Swallows.

"Now play it correctly, guys."

Madden and Jake and the others shift their fingers, play a higher note, one that lives farther up in the chest, closer to the heart than the tummy.

"Excellent, tubas." Mrs. Shadrick grins. "Okay, everyone, pay attention to that section, because it's really easy to slide into that A-flat. In fact, let's mark that. Pencil in a star or something to remind yourself about that tricky turn."

The kids all grab their pencils and scratch on their paper. Madden gulps. His note is still echoing, and it's too low. Too close to his tummy.

"Okay, let's do that again. From the top . . . one-two-ready-PLAY!" The kids start the piece again. Madden's ears are spinny; I can hear them ringing from here. His salty sea level is rising. But Mrs. S is shouting, "It's moving! It's building! Do you feel that?" and he's trying his hardest to blow happy heart notes that his dizzy ears can't hear. He's straining, swimming against the current, trying to play.

That's it. Madden needs an alert.

I nudge his arm with my wet nose.

He keeps playing.

The ocean looms over him, the sea darkening out the sun.

I lick his jeans. They taste fuzzy and metallic, like the small swipes of blood he wipes across their seams after a million pinpricks of his fingers.

He keeps playing.

"I'm feeling it *right here*, guys!" Mrs. S shouts. She points to her heart with her chewed-up stick.

Mrs. S!

I weave through the band room up to her. The music winds and twists and follows my movements, like it's teasing me, chasing me.

I paw Mrs. S's long, swishy skirt. She immediately looks down, then—*slash!* She stops the song with a sharp slice of the air.

The room pulses with leftover music.

"What is it, Zeus?" Mrs. S blinks down at me, her scent full of worry, like a stagnant pond. She looks at Madden. He is pale and clammy.

"Madden, do you need to take a break?"

I can smell Jake sit up straighter from here; he smells superior, like a choice-cut filet in a gooey, too-rich sauce.

"No, ma'am," Madden says. "I just need a few gummy bears is all. Low . . ." His voice trails off, and I sense the sea pulling him further away. I pace at the front of the room. I whine.

Madden chews a handful of gummies.

One of the clarinets asks, "Why does Madden get to eat a snack?"

"Yeah, I'm hungry, too!"

Mrs. S cuts a mean eyebrow, and they silence.

"Kids, let's move on to the next piece. Page sixty-three, please." Paper shifts.

The shadows melt away as Madden's blood sugar swims toward the surface, the light. I sigh, work my way back toward Madden. When I pass Ashvi, she sneaks a hand onto my neck. "Nice work, Zeus," she whispers.

I love her.

I settle back onto my blanket just as Madden is gulping down another lump of gummy bears. Jake leans toward him and barely moves his lips as he whispers, "I can't think of anything more disgusting than eating gummy bears and then immediately playing the tuba. *SO. GROSS.*"

Madden stiffens, his scent scouring like bleach.

"Okay, saxes, altos—put a little more emotion into the song this time, yes?" Mrs. S says, lifting her wrist.

"I did!" a musician from the side of the room mutters.

Mrs. S smiles wearily. "There is no *I* in band."

They begin playing a new tune: soft and gentle like baby spring leaves. Like pale pink flower buds pushing through the wintry claw of once-bare branches. A new beginning.

"Nice," Mrs. S says just over the music. "Do you feel that? *Feel* it. That's pure, right there. We're not going to label it."

Not going to label it?

The song thaws, quiets. Mrs. S sighs. Smiles.

"Did you hear that? Guys. Those instruments sounded like *you*."

The musicians smile at each other, down at their instruments, down at these twists and tangles of brass and wood.

That's *it*!

All this time, I've been going after the things that *help* the music, instead of going after the music itself.

I need to destroy *the instruments*.

⋆ 29 ⋆

MAXIMUM SPLASHAGE

*D*uck. A water fowl. Also, to stoop; to get down quickly. Also, my terrible neighbors.

I personally think two of those different meanings fit together like bacon and my face. Stooping to a duck's level, indeed. So when we study a poem about ducks in Language Arts? Well. I am appalled.

From troubles of the world
I turn to ducks,
Beautiful comical things
Sleeping or curled

This poet, a one Mr. F. W. Harvey, goes on to explain why God fashioned ducks:

He made the comical ones in case the minds of men
Should stiffen and become
Dull, humorless and glum.

If I am understanding these words correctly, *this fellow loves ducks*. I feel it's likely he's never actually met a duck. If he had, this poem would probably be called "An Ode to Muddy Butts."

My jowls curl into a smile. *Mud Butts.* I'm using that next time we're at the pond.

And this afternoon, Page Middle School has a *pep rally.*

As far as I can tell, a pep rally is the closest thing to living inside a vacuum cleaner. It's swirly and squeaky and dusty and loud and confusing and electric and exciting. I blink back the tears all this noise causes. My teeth rattle.

This pack howls and wags and the band plays short pops of songs. The students are foamy and sweaty, and then it's over, and they are turned loose in the hallways. *Turned loose.*

Humans have so many bad ideas.

When we return to the band room, there are only a few minutes left in class. Mrs. S shouts above the fervor: "Great job, but listen. Those instruments look a mess. Let's air those things out, and tomorrow will be a cleaning day. Pile them on the mat over there. Don't forget to tag them! I said *tag it*, Eli! There you go. And yes, grab your mouthpieces and your reeds . . ."

The kids all shuffle to tie a paper tag to their instrument, then add it to the mat. It is a stack of buttons and brass. The bell rings, and the foamy, sweaty kids pour out the door.

In the hallway, Ashvi steps in front of me and Madden, cheeks flushed. She smells shy, hesitant, a sweet scent like the hint of coconut in lip gloss.

"So, uh, no FaceTime practice this afternoon, I guess," she says, tilting her head back through the door at the pile of instruments on the mat.

THE PILE OF INSTRUMENTS ON THE MAT.

Madden shuffles his feet. He is as determined as a leash tug. "No, but I could . . . Icouldcallyouanywaybecausewecouldmaybetalkaboutthearrangementorsomething?"

Ashvi smiles shooting stars. "I'd like that. I really, *really* want to make this duet shine for state. This could lead to something big, like a music scholarship!"

Madden nods. "Me too. I'd really like to win."

Hmmph. We'll see about that.

The air between them is sticky thick like glue, keeping them secured into this conversation, so I know: this is my chance.

I *creeeeeep* back into the room. Mrs. S is banging around in the storage closet, muttering about *stupid ten-year-old instruments* and *no funding for music.* I approach the long mat, covered in shiny music machines.

The smell of the instruments is overpowering: Skunky. Funky. Sixty different vessels for spit. I paw one of the instruments. A saxophone. It's cold: cooler than I expected. It wobbles weirdly.

My nostrils twitch. Humans are able to pinch their noses shut when a smell overwhelms them, but dogs? We can only filter the smell through panting. Slobber. Which is what I do. Gloppy goo drips off my jowls.

I bare my teeth and start chewing on a trombone. Nothing *bone* about it, I'm sorry to say. It tastes metallic, like a toothache. And *yeeouch*—my tongue gets snagged on a slide. I quickly realize that my pointy teeth are largely ineffective against these gadgets. At least, for the amount of time I have.

No, I must use something more powerful.

Call me the Whiz Kid. Mr. Number One. I need to break out the old Yellow Hello. ("Old Yeller" in dog-speak.)

I must use . . . *urine*.

I take a deep breath.

I sniff and circle. Circle and sniff.

At last I find it: the optimum spot to aim for maximum splashage.

I hike my leg . . ..

"ZEUS, YOU STUPID DOG! WHAT ARE YOU DOING?"

Jake is now somehow here, and he lunges across the room at me. I leap and land square in the pile of instruments. I scramble, but my foot gets tangled in a French horn. I clash-clatter through the heap. My foot is pinched, twisted. I yelp. Whine. Fall, face-first.

My backside topples against a knife-sharp something. I feel my skin slice open. Warm red soaks my fur. I whimper.

I'm trapped.

Music won.

Blackness fizzles and pops in my eyesight. I blink. Jake spins away.

Madden and Ashvi lean into my vision. I'm about to get another *bad dog.* It's going to get even worse. I promised myself I wouldn't get any more *bad dog*s after I saw Dave at the prison. And now Madden will return me for sure. I will be *reassigned.* Zeus, Dog of Failure.

But Madden yells, "Mrs. S! Come quick! Zeus is hurt!"

⋆ 30 ⋆

THE ULTIMATE BAD DOG

The next few moments are a blur, like the slide of a trombone:

Mrs. S gently untangles me from the instruments.

Mrs. S and Mr. Nance carry me to a car. It's small and smells like fake pine trees.

Madden calls his mother, "Meet us at the vet."

Ashvi climbs into the back seat of the car. She presses a towel on my cut. She calls her dad. "I'm helping out. Madden says his mother can give me a ride home."

I pant. Pain tastes cold and mushy and dry, like refrigerated canned dog food.

We arrive at the vet.

I limp inside. My back right hip burns.

We are shuffled into a cold room. At last, I have a moment to pry open my eyes. This place is . . . wow. Awful. Stark white. Smells like the fear of ten thousand dogs. This doctor should really invest in some pillows. A rug. A little air freshener. Spruce up the place. Make it less like getting sprayed with the garden hose.

The doctor approaches me with a long, shiny needle. I can practically hear it *ting*, slicing off a sliver of this bright white buzzing light. I gulp. I try not to growl, but my vocal cords have a mind of their own, and they grumble anyway.

I'll be brave for needles. Madden is brave for needles.

The shot stings and burns, and somehow I'm both warm and numb at the same time. I suddenly can't keep my eyes open. They droop. My head nods. My brain swirls. My last thought before I fall into a deep, deep sleep: *I hope I don't drool in front of Ashvi.*

When I wake, it's like I'm inside a machine, a constant, dull hum ringing in my ears. My dry eyes pry open. And everywhere: WHITE. I move my head to see around it, but the whiteness moves with me, scraping along the cold metal table. It's like being lost in a snowstorm.

"I had to shave around where I put the stitches," the doctor says, though I can't see her.

"Well, that's six thousand fewer hairs that'll end up

210

on our floor," Madden's mom says. She laughs at her own joke. She is trying to lighten things up, her scent dry and airy as a feather.

I can't help my glorious mane, I think groggily.

"But he's going to be okay?" Madden asks.

I can't see him because WHITE EVERYWHERE AROUND ME, but he's here! Madden is here. My tail thumps. It drums against the metal table, *thud thud thud*. Madden. And he's worried about me! My heart *ting*s like a xylophone. Just like his.

He puts his hand on my rib cage, and even though I can't see it, I can feel how warm it is.

"Sure, he's going to be okay," the doctor says. "It took a few stitches, but Zeus here is all patched up. He's just going to have to wear this cone for the next several weeks, until his stitches heal a little more."

A *cone*?

A CONE?

My eyes scan the terrifying white plastic all around me: There! And there! And there! My ears tilt forward at their tips, too tall to fit inside this hollow terror. My heart thuds, and I can feel it in my crushed whiskers.

Dear Big Dog in the Sky, I've done it.

I've earned the ultimate *bad dog*. The biggest poke of them all.

I am wearing *a cone*.

⋆31⋆

PITY SMELLS LIKE A FART

I am clunky and uncomfortable in this hunk of plastic. This *cone*. I run into walls. I can't see around corners. But the greatest indignity: I can't get my face close enough to the food bowl to eat. I scooch the bowl around the entire kitchen with the lip of the cone, like one of those big yellow machines that push dirt. I readjust. The hole of the cone fits down over the bowl, but the rim of plastic *thunk*s hollowly on the floor, gagging me, leaving my tongue *juuuuuust* out of reach of the pile of food. I *streeeetch* it, but no. My drool splatters on my food below.

Madden sees this and slides the cone over my head

and it's like all the fresh air and green grass in the world suddenly explode wide around me and I gobblegobblegobble food because, ah, I was so hungry it had been at least two hours since I last ate.

I slurp up water. And then my stitches bite and twitch, and I curl around myself with my teeth bared, ready to chomp—

"Uh-uh-uh, Zeus," Madden says. He slips the cone back over my head, tightens it. "This is why you're in the cone, bud. No messing with those stitches."

I slump. Tuck my tail. Lie on the floor. *Go to school without me*, I say. *I . . . I have a stomachache.*

Madden's eyes soften. He sits cross-legged on the kitchen floor next to me, his knee draping over my ribs. He scratches my neck. And I'm not going to lie: it helps.

"You can't let that cone slow you down, Zeus," Madden says. "You're still the same dog you always were. Just . . . accommodate. You can do it."

Accommodate is not a fancy human word for dating, surprisingly. It means *adapt*.

And here's the thing. That word coming from anyone else would likely swirl around my cone and fly out the back end, like toilet paper getting flushed. But from Madden? He knows all about accommodating for things that could slow you down.

213

So I stand. And as I do, my ears perk toward the hallway, toward the one creaky floorboard. Sock footsteps slide away.

I'm not the only one who heard Madden say that.

Which is good, because I'm not the only one who needed to hear him say it.

I tiptoe into school that morning. If I make myself as wee as possible, they won't see me.

It doesn't work. The pupils swarm me, hands on knees, eyes pooled with worry.

"Aw, Zeus, poor buddy."

"Looooook at 'im!"

"Oh no! The Cone of Shame!"

The only thing worse than the feeling of shame is the feeling of being pitied. There's no way around it: pity smells like a fart, green and growing.

Madden seems to understand how mortifying this is, so he changes what they see. Shifts their focus. Humans are good at doing this. It's the ultimate *oh, you only THINK I threw the stick, but it's actually tucked here behind my back—ha-HA!* "Look at his scar—it looks like a Z!"

Ashvi smiles. "Or a lightning bolt. Zeus, God of Thunder."

God of Thunder! I like that better than God of Chaos.

And it works: the kids' faces pull slowly upward, their foreheads loosen, and they grin.

"Yeah, dude. Totally rockin' that scar."

"You're, like, the toughest guy in the room, Zeus."

"Noice, Z. Tell folks it's a shark bite."

I feel myself uncurl. My tail wags. *Shark bite!*

We go from class to class, and the story of how my injuries happened grows with each bell ring. By the time we reach the end of the day, it seems I fought off a whole gang of kids from a rival school breaking into the band room to steal our instruments. I don't remember any of that, but it sure sounds heroic.

But those stories die when we walk into band and Jake locks eyes with Madden. And Jake's not the only one glaring. It seems others—even Jesus—are squeezing their anger eyes at me. The tightness in this room is shrill and high like a terrible squeaky toy. Those flashes of eyes, those flares of nostrils, remind me that the cone I'm wearing is heavy and hot.

"Class, page forty-two, please," Mrs. S says. She is no-nonsense today. She smells tired, like a blanket covered in fur.

There's a crack zigzagging through the room, sharp

and splintery, fragile as an eggshell. There is a group of friends in here who understand me, who see my scar like a lightning bolt. And there is a group of pupils ready to kick me out of the band, their eyes stinging like hornets. It hangs in the air, the tension between these two groups.

The band begins playing. They are choppy and slow. The woodwinds have a distinct *tuh* sound underneath their notes today, and it sounds like spitting rather than singing. The brass section squeaks and squawks. The drumbeats feel like punches.

"Trumpets at forty-six!" Mrs. S yells over the sound. One trumpet plays right then, instead of at forty-six, and the sound is obvious, a rock stuck in a paw pad. The band member next to that fellow elbows him, mutters, "Nice job."

"Everyone else, stay below the trumpets but keep up your articulation," Mrs. S shouts.

The band usually sounds like a circling owl, hooting hollowly, her majestic wingspan painting moonbeams on the night. But today? Today they sound like those fat, waddling ducks, quacking over their awkward, flappy feet.

Maybe it's just the cone?

They stop playing, and the music limps toward silence. Mrs. S breathes in, long and wordless.

"Well," she says at last. "That was loud and ugly."

So it wasn't the cone.

The pupils all shift and shuffle like they have fleas:

"Mrs. S? I'm a little lost on what the tempo is."

"I can't hear myself play!"

"I think Caleb was hitting the metal frame of the gong, not the actual gong."

"Yeah? Well, I could hit something else!"

"MUSICIANS!"

Mrs. S sometimes shouts over the music, but she's never shouted over the kids. She cracks her knuckles, breathes.

"If you have a tuner, don't forget to turn it off."

It's not the bit of wisdom they were hoping for. It's not a chuckle that says *hey, we're still a team*. They wanted a band joke, her usual pink bubblegum pop of humor. They wanted her to distract them, to change what they saw. To shift their focus to a shark bite instead of a snag of snarly stitches.

I know what's causing this divide. Me. I'm so far from invisible right now. I'm like a tall, tangly barbed-wire fence, keeping this team separated.

Is this how I defeat music? It somehow feels like a hollow win. Like cheating.

The pupils slowly pack away their instruments. It's eerie quiet. Jesus raises his hand.

"Mrs. S? We've still got . . . what? Three weeks before state competition?"

Mrs. S nods. "Yes. But two of those weeks are our winter break."

I didn't think it was possible for the band room to be quieter. Colder. Ashvi sniffles. Is she chilly or . . . ?

Mrs. S's shoulders fall. "Guys," she says at last. "Let me be honest. If you play like that at state, we haven't got a chance."

⋆ 32 ⋆

SIT OUTSIDE THE MUSIC

The next day is the "last day" before winter break, but no one seems to be panicked or alarmed about that term, *last day*. To me, it sounds like the Big Dog is about to call us home to the Big Doghouse in the Sky. But these kids seem downright happy about it, so I chalk up this *last day* term to another poorly thought-out human label.

Each class is rowdier than the one before, and by the time we reach the end of the day, I'm panting from all these weird smells. Madden's blood sugar has dipped and fluttered, but he's stayed on top of it with just a nudge or two from me.

As we walk down the hall toward the band room,

my ears perk toward my name being said inside. "Zeus."

It is followed by the words "doesn't belong here."

My tail tucks.

The voice belongs to the villain himself, Jake Hermann. "Mrs. S, a lot of us don't think Zeus is a good fit for band. Maybe he could sit in the hall while we practice?"

I'm surprised to feel my heart droop alongside my tail. *Sit outside of the music?*

Mrs. S pauses, then replies, "I'm not sure he could do his job from out there, Jake."

I hear the shuffle of Jake crossing his arms through the closed door. He grumbles, "Well, it's not working. Maybe Madden should find a different extracurricular activity."

My stomach knots like a tangled leash. On the one hand, doing that would keep Madden out of the realm of *outstanding*. But on the other hand: no music!

My jowls twitch into a scowl. Caring about *music* again. *Hmmph.*

We swing through the doors at that moment. Jake jumps, burns like too-hot cocoa. But Madden didn't appear to hear him; Madden's scent never changes from the happy-go-lucky, last-day scent of a thrown Frisbee sailing on a sunbeam. He smiles. "Hey," he says to the teacher and the villain.

Jake's eyes flick like a flea between me and Madden, Madden and me. He scowls, turns on his heel, and weaves his way to his tuba.

Other pupils in the class shift their eyes away from me. From Madden. Even Ashvi turns her coppery brown eyes down. Do they agree with the villain? Are they all bad guys, too? Surely not Ashvi . . .

Madden inhales sharply, straightens. His scent has a tinge of storm cloud in it now, the electric sky just before a big rain.

And Mrs. S?

Instead of making Madden feel outstanding, she smiles tiredly. "Take your seat, Madden. We need to jump right in today."

After class, we are *free*, which is a label everyone loves in all its meanings. *Free* may be the skippiest, leapiest, most monstrously marvelous label there is. Madden has shrugged off Jake's glare, and we're gleefully on our way to the car rider line when Jake slides in front of us.

"That dog's a menace," he says, never looking at me. *Menace*. It's a label I'd give to tick bites or a thorny rosebush. Never to some dog.

Wait. *Dog?*

That's me!

This cone suddenly feels like I'm carrying a brick around my neck.

"Don't bring him to state," Jake snarls. I suddenly remember Beef and Vader at Canine College. They often wore similar twists on their faces. "He'll ruin everything."

And here's the thing:

Madden doesn't disagree.

⋆ 33 ⋆

COMFORT IS A
WARM, COZY DOG BED

It turns out winter break is made up of a whole bunch of sleeps and things that look like dog toys and candy but really aren't. First, Madden and his mother drag a sappy dying tree into the house. It is not for chewing. Nor is it for relieving oneself. The moment I hike my leg at it, they both yell, "NO, ZEUS!" Fine. If they want the thing to continue to smell like the too-prickly scent of pine needles, then so be it. (They also do not care for me lapping up water from the bowl they set it in. Humans are weird.)

The shadowy wrinkles on the lieutenant's brow tell me that she doesn't love this messy tree in her neat home, so I'm not sure why she's agreed to it. But

Madden glows and nods at this oversized branch like it's as perfect as a long, paws-up roll in a soft swath of grass.

Then, they pull out all these knotty strings that look perfect for tug-of-war. But *nope*! Another "No, Zeus." They stick one end into a wall, and wow! Lights! They hang these tiny twinkles on the tree. They look like rows of shiny foil candies hidden in the branches. So pretty I want to gobble them up. (I am not allowed to do this, I find.)

And finally, they put balls on the tree. *Balls!* C'mon! They had to know that I'd paw one down, take it gently between my teeth, and drop it on their laps for Fetch. So why they laugh at this suggestion is beyond me. It's embarrassing. I tuck my tail. I mean, *it is a ball.*

The next few days are filled with visitors and food and boxes and singing and laughter and burning candles (humans *set things on fire*! On *purpose*! Inside their *homes*!). It's warm and bright and full of calm, skippy hearts, and all of it together smells like comfort, like a nice drooly chew toy.

I almost forget I'm wearing this godforsaken cone. Almost.

And Madden almost forgets the thing he carries, too. He stops sometimes and whispers, "I wish Nana and PopPop could come," and his pulse droops to an adagio tempo. *Adagio* is a label I learned in band. It means *slow*. The lieutenant shifts, shuffles, clears her throat. Madden is soon distracted by tubas and flutes and Ashvi.

Ashvi. The best parts of winter break are when Ashvi comes over and they practice at the pond. She and Madden practice almost every day, and by *practice*, I mean they talk a lot and harmonize their laughter and their heartbeats, and sometimes they even play their instruments. Ashvi talks a lot about "nailing the duet" and "winning state" and "helping me get a music scholarship to college." And Madden nods and glows and agrees. HE AGREES.

But when we're alone, Madden still tells me that he thinks Ashvi only likes us because of the duet. "Once we're done with state, she won't hang out with us anymore, Z. Just watch."

Today, Ashvi bends over her flute case, then straightens suddenly. The wind ripples across the pond, and her hair lifts around her face. "I forgot to tell you—last night when I was practicing, I found a test strip in my instrument case. It made me think of you." She smiles like blooms of honeysuckle, and Madden sizzles to a crisp. I could sneeze and blow his ashes away.

"I love you, Ashvi." That's all you have to say, dude.

He doesn't say it.

Humans don't know themselves very well.

It's cold at the pond today, so cold the ducks are hiding somewhere warm. *I don't miss them*, I tell myself. *This peace is nice.* I think Madden likes it here because there is no adult barking orders at him. I know young humans like that kind of peace. I personally find a lack of orders bewildering.

Madden and Ashvi remove their gloves, puff on their red hands. They play a few warm-up scales, and Ashvi chuckles. "I hope I can play out here. I can barely feel my upper lip."

The coals in Madden's chest glow red again at the mention of Ashvi's upper lip. He smells as smoky as a campfire.

Seriously, dude. Tell her I. LOVE. YOU. It's easy. Watch.

I stand and soften my big browns at Ashvi, making my eyes like puddles. I flutter my eyelashes, lift my jaw, and wag my tail veeeery gently. *Hey, girl. I love you.*

Ashvi cocks her head at me, the red cold just under her skin warming and thawing as her grin grows. She reaches into my cone and scritches my neck.

"Aw, hey, Zeus! How're you doing today? I love you, buddy." She plants the tiniest of kisses on the tip of my cold nose, and my heart sings a small three-note ditty.

I shoot a single raised eyebrow at Madden. *And THAT, my dude, is how it's done.* I lie back down in the crunchy grass.

They begin to practice, the warmth of their melodies making them forget the cold. Their notes echo off the water, sing into the sky. The gray clouds sway, the grass jimmies like maracas. The bare trees whistle, their claws snatching at patches of fog and dancing with them like ribbons.

Ashvi sits suddenly, looks at the collar strapped around her wrist. "Oh! It's almost four—I gotta run! I can't believe how the time flew by today."

She scrambles to pack up her flute. I hear that label a lot from humans: *time*. Humans place a lot of importance on this idea. And here's what I've noticed about music: it makes humans forget about time. The slices of a day that humans use to mark their march forward don't seem to exist—at least, not in the same way— inside a song. Music expands and fills and paints a space, and people spin like the orbs in Madden's room inside it, suspended in the moment.

Ashvi clicks her instrument case shut and hops on her seat to face Madden.

"Madden, listen. You know I love Zeus, right?"

I smile. Wink at her.

But Madden gulps, and his voice comes out thin and unsteady, like pond ice. "Yeah?"

"So I don't know how to tell you this, but . . . well, some of the band members are upset with him. They don't want him to come to state. I mean, he keeps acting out, and he's wearing that obvious cone, and . . ." Her voice blows away on the breeze. "I mean, they're wondering: He could just stay home for a few hours, right?"

This cone feels heavier and itchier than ever. I lie down.

Madden can go to state without me. I will be okay letting him out of my sight for a while, yes? I can do this for him and Ashvi. *Ashvi?* Her asking this hurts worse than walking on gravel. I can—

WHO AM I KIDDING? NO WAY CAN I ALLOW THAT TO HAPPEN! CURSE YOU, BAND! CURSE YOU, MUSIC!

Anger smells like the gritty exhaust fumes of a big bus. Madden breathes that out now. I look up at him with big, soft eyes—the ones humans can't say no to—but he won't even look at me. His words are clipped short as toenails. "And what do *you* think?"

Ashvi's teeth grind like machinery. Her shoulders

228

rise, then fall. "I just . . . I wonder . . . just in case . . . should I start practicing the duet with Jake?"

Her label up until now was *perfect*. This doesn't feel *perfect*.

Madden grips my leash too tightly and tugs me away.

⋆ 34 ⋆

STACCATO (IT'S A LABEL
I LEARNED IN BAND)

Madden twirls a brand-new fuzzy yellow tennis ball in his fingertips. Nothing, and I mean NOTHING, smells as good as a brand-new fuzzy yellow tennis ball. It is the smell of joy.

He *hurls* the ball, and it sails across the sky like a tiny sun. I spring off my back legs like a jackrabbit. But this godforsaken cone blocks what I can see from the corners of my eyes, and the ball *thwack*s the side of the plastic, just below my left ear.

The ball bounces, rolls. I chase it. But this cone stops me from putting my face close enough to the ground to scoop up the ball in my teeth. I end up pushing the ball through the grass with the lip of the cone. The ball—the JOY—is *just* out of reach.

Staccato. It's a label I learned in band. It means notes that are played sharply, distinctly, with a pause between each one. The notes are separate.

This ball and me? *Staccato.*

Madden sighs. Drops cross-legged onto the yard. Picks at the brown grass and tosses a handful into the wind.

I'm getting it wrong. I'm getting everything wrong. I can't even pick up a ball! If my dad could see me now, he'd tuck his tail with disappointment. Not invisible. Not successful. *Reassignment* is as near as my whisker tips.

I'm "nailing" my mission, as Ashvi says, but I'm failing at everything else. I don't know what that means; my mission is still my priority, right? But I will surely be reassigned, just as the lieutenant was.

I sit next to Madden. The ball sits far away from us. I feel like the sun is far away.

Madden drapes an arm over my shoulder, and the weight of it makes me feel lighter. Funny how that is.

"Zeus, can you start making better choices?"

This confuses me, because I feel like I've been making excellent choices. My choices focus on my mission: keeping Madden invisible. Invisible is *safe.* But still I nod. *I . . . think so?*

231

"Can you stop acting out in band, Zeus? Can you, boy?"

This question feels like an itch in a place I can't reach with my back paw. I want to get a *Whoossa good boy?* from Madden. I want to make him happy. More than anything.

But my job is to *help* him. He must stop playing music. I see what the lieutenant sees: it's too risky for him to play. The tuba is heavy and takes so much effort. It makes his blood go wild as wolves. Madden wants to play in the band, and I want him to stop. Dave's words from the evaluation ring in my pointy ears: Zeus should be "wisely disobedient."

I must always do what's best for Madden. Even if it's not what he wants. Even if it's not easy.

"This is important to me, Zeus. I need you to stop hurting the band. The lieutenant—she won't let me go to state without you. I know it. I need you, Z."

My heart twists and frays like a tug-of-war towel. Because Madden says he needs me, but he needs me for *music*. This is exactly what he thinks Ashvi is doing; he thinks she's only friends with him because of their duet. Now he's doing the same thing to me—keeping me around so he can play the music he wants to play. *Ironic* is a fancy human word for *wow, that hurts a lot.*

The ball sits across the yard. Madden sits so close

he's leaning against me. But both are *staccato*.

Separate.

Detached.

Sharp.

At school the next day, we pass Ashvi in the hall. She pinks, gives us a half-hearted wave, and tries to make eye contact with Madden. He ignores her as if he's a cat and she's, well, any of the billions of things cats pretend to ignore. We pass by. I look back over my shoulder. Ashvi slumps against her locker, her scent like a bruised peach.

★ 35 ★

I'M WITH THE BAND

Madden pushes numbers on his phone twelve times that night but huffs and hangs up before the screen lights. Thirteen times. Fourteen. He growls. On try fifteen, he sucks in a huge breath, punches in each one of the numbers, and pauses. I hear Ashvi's voice—"Hello?"—and see her face pop up on the tiny blue screen.

Madden suddenly smells as confident as a newly tarred road. "Listen. You want to win state. *I* want to win state. So hear me out. I have an idea."

The next day, I find myself in Madden's bathroom, Ashvi's colorful fingertips twiddling all around me.

Each of her fingernails is painted a different shade, so I'm mesmerized watching them; it's like being spun inside cotton candy. Sometimes she scratches me, and my tongue lolls out over my jaw. Her scritches are perfect, of course: strong and confident. They are so different from the odd, fingernail-less scritches from the lieutenant.

Ashvi loosens and gently lifts the cone over my head and *ahhh*. It's like breathing full into my belly again. Humans often make this satisfied sigh when they peel sweaty socks off their feet; that sigh is how it feels to have that heavy chunk of plastic lifted off my neck.

"Are you sure about this?" Ashvi asks, holding a bright yellow paintbrush over my cone.

Madden nods once. "Yes. I think." Hope and doubt, side by side.

Ashvi smiles like the flash of a dragonfly wing. "Glitter me."

Madden hands her a tube filled with shiny golden star chips, and she sprinkles it over the drying yellow paint.

"Okay. Let's make the tubes and valves." Ashvi rolls up strips of yellow felt and binds them together with hot glue. It smells like burning hair. Then she twists and folds pieces of yellow construction paper to look like the buttons on a musical instrument. This creation gets attached together, then attached to my cone. All of it gets a coating of gold star chips. *Glitter.*

I get so excited about all the shiny, I sneeze—*wachoo!* A poof of gold blooms like a cloud and settles over everything in this bathroom. Gold sink, gold toilet. Fancy! Ashvi giggles sweet as lollipops. Madden swipes a hand over his hair and attempts a smile. I can practically hear him thinking about how the lieutenant is going to react to all these glitter chips.

"Did you get a new vest?" Ashvi asks. Madden nods and pulls a black vest out of a cardboard box, followed by a black leash.

Vest goes on. Leash gets clipped. New, fabulous cone slides over my head. The new creation, these twists of valves and tubes, gets pinned to my vest.

"Voilà!" Ashvi says. She turns her palms toward me. They sparkle, coated in glitter.

Madden tilts his head. His scent lightens slightly; it shifts from worried green onion to pleased green grass. He grins.

"This might just work, Ashvi. We might win now! Zeus, look!"

Madden tugs my new leash and I follow his command, *turn.* I spin, and there, in the glass, is the other dog, Glass Zeus. Madden always says that's me. And today I want to believe him.

Because Glass Zeus looks like a *musician.*

I look like a musician!

I look like I'm part of the band!

Ashvi has turned my cone into a tuba. I fit right in—no obvious red vest, no bright blue leash, and a brand-new, shiny glitter tuba.

My chest puffs with pride. I lift my chin, turn, and look at Glass Zeus from another angle. I am definitely a musician. *Wouldja get a load of that handsome fella? That is no mutt right there!*

My heart swells, and it fills with music, a melody of strong, thumping joy, like a Sousa march.

But—*oh!*

I blink.

Music?

I'm not supposed to be a *part* of the music.

I'm supposed to stop it.

I am supposed to keep Madden invisible. Invisible = safe.

I'm supposed to thwart the *outstanding.*

How can I stop Madden from being outstanding, when I want it for myself, too?

We make our way downstairs, each of us with our instruments. The lieutenant looks up from her blue palm screen.

And she does something I've never heard her do before.

She *laughs*. A deep, hearty belly laugh.

Her laugh is like jazz, dipping and swaying, full of surprises. Chaos.

"Zeus, you look fantastic!" she says.

More handsome than a poodle on grooming day, if I do say so!

The lieutenant takes a swig of syrupy orange juice. Based on her pursed lips, she's trying not to say something to Madden; it's the same effect of a whining dog trying not to bark. Finally, she says, "How's your blood sugar? Need any juice for the ride?"

She tilts the bottle his way. Madden shudders. Scowls like he's smelled rotten meat. "*Mom*. No. I hate OJ. You know that."

The lieutenant burns with an apologetic scent. But she doesn't say *I'm sorry*, and I don't know why. Humans say *I'm sorry* only a fraction of the time when they smell like *I'm sorry*. "Let's go. It's about an hour's drive to Princeton."

The three of us pile in the back seat of the lieutenant's truck, me perched between Madden and Ashvi. I can tell they are happy to have me between them by the way they slide their eyes at each other when the other one isn't looking. It's like sitting between two boxes of roly-poly marbles.

The truck grumbles for a long while, then stops. We pile out of the car at a school that smells quite a lot like our school, Page Middle. But it's not. This school is much, much larger than ours. And the kids! They are everywhere. Swarms of them, like armies of ants. All of them carrying instruments. It's bizarre, and it confuses my nose.

A large fellow mushrooms over a stool at the front door, clipboard in hand. He does a double take when he sees me, grins, then laughs. I lift my chin. The bell of my tuba sways.

"No pets, kids," he says.

I shake my head, jangling my leash. *I'm with the band.*

"He's a service dog," the lieutenant says.

The dude narrows his eyes. "What's he do?"

Ashvi steps forward. "It's actually illegal to ask that." *I love her.* A clog of kids toting black instrument cases has formed behind us.

But the lieutenant loudly states, "He's a diabetic alert dog." Madden shifts, burns like the scent of charred marshmallow over a fire.

"Oh yeah, I sees that now on this here list. Go on in, then."

We walk inside, and everyone who spots me smiles,

giggles, chuckles, points. I grin, my tongue loose and floppy. My tail wags.

"Hey, Zeus, nice getup!"

"Dude, is that your dog? Awesome!"

"Aw, look! He has a *tuba*!"

Jesus is filling a water bottle in the massive school lobby, and when he sees me, his face splits into a smile. "Hey, Zeus!" He holds a fist out to Madden, who pounds it with his own fist. "That costume is exceptional, dude."

Unless I am mistaken (and let's face it, I rarely am), *exceptional* is a fancy human word for PRACTICALLY OUTSTANDING.

My stomach tangles like the cord Madden uses to listen to his blue screen.

Practically *outstanding*. There's that word again, and this time, it applies to me.

I am both overjoyed and saddened, and I'm tail-chasing confused by this mix of emotions. I've worked since I was a pup to blend in, to be an invisible helper, a quiet, loyal, service dog, just like the dogs in my bloodline. They have counted on me to be just like them—unseen and unheard—since I was a tiny pup. Stayed as invisible as a tail, I have. I've done everything by the commands, order by order. And yet here I am, being *exceptional*. One step away from *outstanding*.

This is a label I'm not supposed to have. A tag I'm not supposed to wear.

This will never do. I mutter, *Me, exceptional?*

Oh. My. Dog. Is that Zeus Zagnut Zealousness I see?

My full name. No one here knows my full name. I turn, but the bulky tuba—the *cone*—prevents me from seeing who said it.

I spin.

And there he stands, all towering four feet of him, a wall of muscle and bulk. I look up into the scruff of whiskers under his chin. (He always had great facial hair, drat him. He was *born* with a doggone mustache.)

Beef.

He wears a navy-blue vest with the symbols for *K-9 Unit* on the side. He is apparently here with the security team, helping keep these thousands of band kids safe.

We circle one another. Give each other's hind end a sniff, a *long* sniff, a *deeeeep* sniff, trying to see who can outsniff the other, who can sniff the longest. Rude, yes. Obnoxious, absolutely. But I can't let Beef win. I can sniff longer. And, hey—don't judge. I've seen humans do this with handshakes.

At last we curl toward one another, face-to-face. My face to Beef's chest, more accurately. His whiskers twitch. His left eyebrow cocks, then his right. Then he explodes into full-on laughter, barking and wheezing and gagging. His eyes water.

Is that—a CONE? Oh, Zeus, whatEVER have you been into?

He is laughing so hard, he doesn't hear my reply: *It's a tuba.*

Hooo boy, Zeus. I knew you'd go and make a fool of yourself in the real world. I just didn't realize how spectacularly you'd fail. A CONE! He paws at his face and sneezes, he's laughing so hard. *I am so glad my human took this ridiculous side gig today. I got to see Zeus Zagnut Zealousness, in a CONE!*

This isn't ridiculous, I mutter, *this is band.* But I don't think he hears me. I drop into a sit. My whole life is so out of tune right now.

Word on the wind is that you're about to be reassigned, Beef says. *All the dogs from Canine College are talking about it.*

All the dogs? I gulp. Of course they are. Dogs are terrible at keeping secrets. We can't lie; our hearts are too pure. If Beef asked one of the dogs still in school how my evaluation went when *he* went back for *his* evaluation . . .

Yep. Beef knows.

He leans over me, growls into my pointy ear. *Everyone at Canine College thought you were so special.*

242

But I knew better. You were always too practical to be exceptional. I knew you'd fail. It'll happen. That reassignment—it'll happen.

"Come, Beef!"

Beef stiffens, turns, trots away behind his human.

My throat tightens, and tears prick my eyes. This day cannot get any worse.

Madden sways next to me, his blood steely and dark. "I—I can't find my instrument."

Ashvi shakes her head. "What?"

"My tuba. It's gone."

★ 36 ★

I SMELL TUBA

"Your tuba can't be *gone*," Ashvi says, scurrying and looking under and around things. "It was *right here*. Right next to my flute."

"I know," Madden says, gulping. His blood isn't dangerous, not yet, but it's falling so fast, it's like watching the ocean recede and swell, recede and swell. "But it's not there now."

Mrs. Shadrick's jaw tightens. "You need to find it quickly, Madden. We're on in ten minutes. If you can't find it, I'll need to ask Jake to perform the duet with Ashvi."

All three sets of eyes slide toward me. *I didn't do it this time, I promise!*

Madden and Ashvi scurry around like mice, asking others if they've seen an extra tuba lying around.

"Oh, hon," says one band mom. She sweeps her hand over the massive lobby, over a maze of black instrument cases. Thousands of them. "Good luck finding that in here."

I can find it, I murmur. I say it because I know they can't hear me.

"Five minutes!" Mrs. S shouts. "We go on in five minutes! Line up, Page band!"

And I can. I *can* find it. I know this. All I have to do is open my nostrils and breathe. I can find anything of Madden's. His scent is my whole purpose.

But should I?

I've spent every moment since meeting Madden trying to destroy the thing that makes him outstanding: *music*. I've failed over and over again. And here is my chance to keep him under the radar. Invisible. Safe.

We could head home. Have a quiet afternoon of chasing ducks and throwing pebbles into ponds. It'd be so easy.

The Page band lines up at the auditorium door, their instruments out of their cases and lifted to their chests, ready to walk in as one. Madden and Ashvi aren't with them. My shoulders droop. This cone—my tuba—is heavier than ever.

I've been told my whole life that being invisible is a noble goal. I've tried doing it. Worked hard at it, harder than anyone. *Disappear, Zeus.* And then today, suddenly, I *wasn't* invisible. I was part of something bigger than myself. I was part of *the band*.

And I loved it.

I loved feeling special. Unique. And yet a part of something bigger than just me.

The strength of the pack is the wolf, and the strength of the wolf is the pack. Dave said that when I graduated. And now I think I understand. That is how it feels to be in band.

Madden's heart races like a drumroll. I can't look him in the eyes; they are filled with pain and panic. His scent is fiery, smoky, smoldering.

"Three minutes, Page!"

That's it. I close my eyes, flare my nostrils, inhale deeply—

—and sort through all the scents lingering nearby: Salami. Wax off a cheese wheel. An apple core in a bin. Used Kleenex. Hair products and deodorant and makeup and toothpaste. Nervous sweat from a thousand middle school performers. SO MUCH INSTRUMENT SPIT.

Then I find it. I smell *tuba*. Madden's tuba. I labeled it Beef. That's not exactly right.

I tug Madden's pants leg, and he instinctively picks up the leash he dropped several minutes ago. I *puuulllll* him toward a door. On it is a picture of a woman in a dress. Behind it is . . . *human* smell. The worst kind.

I paw at the door.

"Zeus, *what*?"

I rake my toenails across the metal handle. Whimper.

"Zeus, we don't have time for—oh! Is something in there, bud? My tuba?"

Madden shoots a look at Ashvi, who swings the door wide with a shove. I plow inside, pulling Madden behind me. A row of girls at the sink gasp and shout, "Hey!" "Get out of here!"

But I pull Madden to the far stall, the wide one, and to the chair that is squat and white and smells awfulawfulawful. (Honestly, humans. *Indoors?* You are animals.)

Wedged behind it, atop a rusty stain on the grubby tile floor, sits a tuba case.

"You found it, Zeus!" Ashvi says. "Good boy! Also, omigosh, so gross. But good boy!"

Madden snatches it, and he, Ashvi, and I run back to the lobby.

Madden flings the case open and frantically pieces the tuba together. Ashvi exhales, nods, smiles. She takes her flute from its case and lifts it to her chest.

"One minute," Mrs. S says, but she's smiling now, too. Her hand is on the door to the auditorium, ready to fling it open wide.

Madden gets his tuba assembled, stands erect, lifts his instrument to his chest . . .

. . . and sways.

He is deep in a dark, briny sea. His blood sugar has bottomed out.

★ 37 ★

WIDE LIFE

Madden plunges into a deep, hollow, curling wave. A quickly crashing wave. The stress of performing, of losing his instrument, is causing this plummet to be worse—*faster*—than most. His vision clouds. His skin grows pale, clammy. Cold, shivery sweat dots his upper lip.

I nudge him. He nudges me back with his knee. "Not *now*, Zeus," he whispers through gritted teeth. "We don't have time for your shenanigans."

Shenanigans? Dude, I'd douse you with cold spray from the garden hose if I could.

I lick his pants. Tug them with my teeth. They taste

like dirty laundry. I don't know the last time these black pants have been washed. *Blech.* But I keep at it.

I nudge and whimper and spin in circles. Madden blinks, gulps.

His eyes connect with mine.

Madden, you need sugar.

Then, dear sweet Dog above, it's like he heard me: he nods.

There is no time here, now, to test his sugar levels with his plastic contraptions. He reaches into his pocket. Grabs a handful of gummies. Starts chewing.

But here's the thing about human teeth. They're dull as pebbles. He grinds and grinds, trying to gulp down sugar, but it's not working fast enough. His sea grows taller, darker.

I have to do it. Madden is going to be so mad at me, but it's the only way. I jerk the leash out of his hand, take a sniff of the air, and find the lieutenant nearby. I weave through the crowd until I locate her. Our eyes lock. The moment she sees me, she knows: *Follow.*

I lead her back to Madden. She sees him cold and clammy, sweating. Chewing.

"In we go, Page!" Mrs. S yells. She flings open the door, and the first few band members file into the darkened auditorium.

The lieutenant drops the bag she carries. Touches

250

Madden lightly on the shoulders. "Madden, you need to sit down."

Inside her bag is her bottle of orange juice from this morning. Madden *hates* orange juice. Has ever since he had to practice stabbing that orange with a needle. But it's the only thing that will work fast enough. I paw at it. Whine.

More Page band members stream inside. It is almost our turn to walk.

Madden shakes his head. Mumbles around the mouthful of gummy goo. "I can't, Mom. I've been practicing that duet for weeks! I want this. I want to win this. And I can't let my band members down."

They don't see me pawing, whining. I'm not supposed to do this—a service dog is never supposed to do what I'm about to do—but I see no other way. So I do it. I let down my invisibility. I BARK, raw and loud.

They look my way. The lieutenant scoops up the orange juice, unscrews the top, hands it to Madden.

"If there's anything I understand, it's not letting your team down," the lieutenant says. "Drink this. *Hurry.*"

The band is now halfway inside the auditorium. Madden's part of the line begins to move; he walks toward the auditorium door. I am by his side, step for step. He tips back the orange juice, scowls. Shudders.

Gulps. Swipes at his now-sticky face. "Ugh!"

But almost immediately, a ray of sun brightens his dull skin, beaming from behind his wall of seawater. He is swimming his way out of this curling wave.

We are at the door now, just about ready to go inside. He thrusts the empty bottle at his mom.

She glances at it, looks up at him with glassy, salty eyes. Nods. "I want to do a better job protecting you than I did your dad." Her voice is whispery and wavery, like our rippling pond. "I just want you to live a long, healthy life, M."

Madden inhales, swimming further into the sun. His face softens at her, soft as a perfect swirl of ice cream. "I can't control how long my life is, Mom. But I can control how wide."

And Madden and I turn and march inside, our tubas and our chins held high.

⋆ 38 ⋆

THE DUET BECOMES A TRIO

We, the musicians from Page Middle School, shuffle into the cool, dark auditorium, down the long aisles, up the stairs, and onto the stage. It is a long walk, all trotting hearts and raw nerves. I hear whispers about my instrument on the way down the aisle: "Is that a dog?" "With a tuba?" "Oh my."

I'd forgotten what being onstage under all these hot, bright lights feels like. It feels as obvious as a flea collar.

Music stands and chair legs scrape the wooden stage as we take our seats. Sheet music flutters, shuffles. The musicians squint into deep dark, seeking friendly parent faces. Nerves pop like bubble wrap into giggles and nudges. Mrs. Shadrick raises her hand, and all the shuffling and scraping silences.

Such power! She is *business*. Still.

"Whenever we want to improve something, we add music to it," Mrs. Shadrick says into the dark. She's not shouting, but the auditorium is so large and quiet, her voice is amplified. "And yet art and music are often the last to get funding in schools. Demand that your education system fund an excellent music program."

Mrs. S smiles down at her notes. "But you know that. You're here today. Thank you, parents, for supporting the arts, and for loving your kids through sounding really bad. Musicians have to blow their way through awful to get to awesome."

There is laughter in the darkness. Mrs. S inhales. Tilts her chin into the light. "We are the Page Middle School musicians."

Mrs. S lifts her hands palms up, and the students raise their instruments. Then there is this . . . *pause* . . . this rest, when the music hasn't yet started, and the notes linger just on the edge of each musician's breath. It is *anticipation*. It is *expectation*. That pause is filled with promise.

Mrs. S whips a wrist to her left, and the cymbals crash, roll. It is a command: *Listen, Zeus*. I sit taller. Tears prick my eyes.

The bass drum in back rumbles, then growls. The

sound of mallet on drum feels like Earth itself, roll-
ing through space. I think of the orbs that float from
Madden's ceiling. A shiver marches down my spine, the
hairs standing on end.

The triangle zings like butterfly wings. The xylophone tiptoes in. And then the flutes skip along. The
trombones slide up alongside this piece, wedge themselves in. The saxophones sneak up, creeping along like
shadows, and pounce!

My every whisker, every tooth, every toenail listens
to this music. *Feels* it. And it's like the music hears *me*,
too. Like it knows my emotions and it tickles them,
gives them belly rubs and scratches and *attaboy*s.

Jesus stands. It's time for his trumpet solo. He arches
his back, lifts his instrument, and *wails*. He crams every
bit of himself through that tiny mouthpiece, through
that bell, and out into a song. His trumpet tells my
heart what to feel, my brain what to think, my stomach
how to churn. It gets down inside my gut and spins me
around, leaving me dizzy and dancey.

My tail wags. *Stop it, tail.* But as always, tails don't
listen. They don't have ears.

The band fades back in behind this solo like a pat of
melting butter. The music dips and sways, a flag skipping on the wind. Then Madden and Ashvi stand.

Madden is as steady as Earth.

Ashvi begins playing. Her flute is a dragonfly, sleek and slivery, darting to and fro, her stained-glass wings *just* skimming the surface of the water. Her buzz is enough to stir a sleeping frog: Madden's tuba. The frog is grumbly, grumpy from being awoken with such a rude buzz-by, but he bellows when he sees the dragonfly. The frog chases the sleek needle of a bug from lily pad to lily pad, splashing and galumphing, long legs flapping, sleek skin shining. Together, they are SPRING.

My heart swells like the throat of the frog.

Uh-oh. NO, ZEUS, I command myself. *NO!*

I swallow the temptation to croak out a song.

I blink, and just beyond Madden, I see Jake. He's sitting, of course. Not playing. But his fingers move along the buttons of his tuba the same as Madden's, as if he were. Jake's heart pulls toward the music, and suddenly, I understand.

Jake is invisible. He's miserable. (And I don't think humans made a mistake when they made those two labels rhyme. They are much the same.) All Jake wants is to feel special, too. To be seen. He wants to be the frog.

My throat swells again. I could just . . . *sing*.

NO, ZEUS!

And Beef? He's wrong. He's *been* wrong. I haven't

failed. I am not a failure! I'm very good at what I do: keeping Madden healthy. I'm just not good at being invisible.

I'm not good at being invisible.

And that's when it happens: the shimmy starts in the very tip of my tail and works its way through my fur toward my wet nose, like fingernails scratching me backward, my hairs on end. It reaches my vocal cords, and I feel them warming with a soft, subtle whine. *MMMmmmMMM*. My tags jangle.

I can't contain it.

Ashvi's flute hits a high C, Madden's tuba bottoms out with a low E, and I toss my nose into the air and *hooooowlllll. AAAAAARRRoooOOOOO!*

I don't care what the others think. This duet needs to become a trio. I can feel it. My head tosses back— *how-howw-hoOOOOOoowwlllll!* My cone amplifies the sound—I have my very own instrument!

Madden smiles behind his mouthpiece, and that smile spins through his tuba and out into his music until the whole room can hear it: he is OUTSTANDING.

That is his label! *Outstanding*. It means all sorts of things, that label. And that's okay. Better than okay. *Aaaaaa-aaaa-OOOOOOooooooUTSTANDING!*

The other Page musicians do their jazzy chaos thing, and riff off a few extra notes and tones to accentuate my addition. We are a chorus of bullfrogs and butter-flies, rays of sun and swishing trees.

The piece winds down. Silence falls. It is still so hot, so bright here onstage. Then the audience explodes with tail-wagging applause.

Mrs. S raises her hands again, palms up. The Page Middle musicians stand. I stand. She folds her fingers down. The musicians all bend at the waist. It's swirly confusing.

Madden slides his eyes my way. "Bow, Zeus," he whispers from the corner of his mouth.

I follow Madden's command. I drop the front half of my body into a deep bow. Tail high. Eyes closed.

The audience wags louder.

★ 39 ★

NOT JUST
ANOTHER PRETTY FACE

We file out of the dark auditorium, and when we reach the lobby, Madden pales again. Sways. Before I can even give him a nudge, Mrs. S sees him, and she gently grabs his elbow and guides him to the front of the concession stand line.

"I got someone with diabetes here!" she shouts to the people behind the counter. "Get me some lemonade, please. Quickly!"

Madden's scent is sprinkled with red pepper flakes of embarrassment. But he nods and accepts the help. HE ACCEPTS THE HELP. He leans over the counter himself and says, "One hot dog, too, please."

Madden glances at his CGM monitor. He leans

against the cool brick wall.

The lieutenant weaves through the crowd. Her brow is wrinkled like crinkly cardboard, and her whole scent is shouting, *Are you okay, Madden?* But she glances at me, and I give a reassuring look that says, *If he weren't okay, I'd let you know.* And so she doesn't ask. Somehow, she knows not to ask.

"You were phenomenal, Mad!" she says. She wraps her arms around him. She's tall, and he's skinny, and those arms almost wrap around him twice. "PopPop would say you got major chops, son!"

They both laugh. The lemonade and the hot dog appear, and Madden gulps the drink, face wincing with sour. He takes a couple quick bites of the hot dog, and I know he needs something to balance out all this sugar he's taken in so quickly. The hot dog smells like heaven in a bun: salty, juicy, greasy. My nostrils quiver. I lick a drop of drool off my jowl.

Madden laughs. He squats and looks me in the eye. I hear the thrum of his heart: low and strong like his tuba. He then offers me the other half of the hot—

GULP!

It's gone so fast I barely taste it, that hot dog. I hope it's not made from *actual dogs*, because it's the most delicious thing I've ever tasted. But the scent lingers on my tongue, and I smile. Pant. I hope I burp a lot so I can taste it some more.

The lieutenant laughs, too. "And Zeus, your performance was great! I think you're as good at singing as you are at scent detection. Have you been practicing?"

Thank you. And, well, yes. I practice with Madden and Ashvi almost daily at the pond with my astounding barks.

Mrs. S smiles at me, and I gotta be honest: the three of them all looking at me with shiny up-smiles instead of shadowy down-frowns is maybe even better than a *whoossa good boy?*

"You know, at the beginning of the school year, I used to worry about Madden all the time," Mrs. S says. The lieutenant blinks at her, and Madden's eyebrows pull into a question mark. This is apparently new information.

"I used to be so concerned. *Does he feel okay? Is band too much for him? Does he look off?* But now that Zeus is with us, I don't worry about him nearly as much. Zeus isn't just a great singer. He's very good at his job."

But the best part of her saying this? Picture it: Beef is just behind her. He hears every word, too, based on the way his silly jowls droop into a deep scowl.

So I'm not just another pretty face? I say, and I wink at Beef.

Beef looks like he's wearing one of those collars that stun you if you run out of the yard. He blinks. I decide to be the bigger dog.

It was good seeing you again, Beef. I hope you're enjoying your assignment. I love mine.

I love mine? That's the first time I've said that very most important of all human labels, *LOVE*, about Madden and the lieutenant. I smile at them. *I love mine.*

Madden hugs my neck, squeezing in around my awkward tuba. The lieutenant reaches down and scratches behind my ears. And here's the thing: she has *fingernails*. Glorious, itchy-scratchy fingernails, like whatever had been causing her to gnaw at her own fingertips wasn't making her do that now. She scratches, and I cock my head. It feels so splendid that I lean into the scratch, my right leg thumping the floor. She shakes her fingers, and a huge poof of Zeus fur floats off them.

"He is pretty good at this job, isn't he?" the lieutenant says.

Madden adjusts my tuba, then scratches the secret spot *juuuust* under my chin that only he knows about. "He's more than pretty good, Mom. He's outstanding."

* * *

A trophy is brassy and shiny, just like a musical instrument, although no one blows into it. Apparently, what you do with it: you hold it above your head and shriek. This seems odd to me, but humans make no sense whatsoever.

We, the members of the Page Middle band, hold the shiny brassy trophy over our heads, and we pose for pictures while the air explodes like mini bursts of lightning all around us. No one else seems to be freaked out by this unnatural indoor thunderstorm, however, so I just stand pert and alert, shackles raised.

"Hey, Zeus, get up here," Jesus yells. "Right up front!"

And I do. I move to the front of the group with my tuba. Jesus scritches my neck—*ahhhhh*—and he smiles at me, then Madden. "Looks like it took *four* of us to win state, not three. Right, Z? Now, smile!"

I smile, and drool a bit when everyone yells "Cheeeese!" because CHEESE WHERE?!

The weird indoor lightning continues. *Pop! Flash!* "Cheeeese!" "Wooohoooo!"

The strength of the pack is the wolf, and the strength of the wolf is the pack. Now that I'm in the band, I get it. I am with the band. I am part of the pack. And we're

263

both stronger because of it.

The band leans in. They smell like joy and music spit and hormones. They smile and whoop as they crowd around me.

Outstanding, *visible* me.

★ 40 ★

SUPERSTAR!

Superstar.

Super. To excel, to be the best. First in class.

Star. A heavenly body. Shines at night. You know, "Twinkle, twinkle . . . ?" We play it in band.

When Ashvi finds me in the chaos post-competition, that's what she calls me: a superstar. "Zeus, look right here!" She waves a folded, colorful piece of paper at me, points. "Your name is in the band program! You're a superstar!"

Superstar! That's exactly what Dave promised I'd become, back at the Canine College graduation. And I did it! With the band, I did it.

Ashvi hugs my neck, and then she skips away,

trailing my heart and Madden's heart behind her like two colorful ribbons.

Madden shoots a look at Mrs. S, who shrugs.

"You put Zeus in the program?" he asks.

"Of course!" Mrs. S smiles at me, and I wink. "He's our mascot." Then she looks at Madden. "I'd like for you to audition for jazz band next year, okay?"

His scent changes to bursting joyous surprise, like the rubbery powder scent inside a popped balloon. But then his eyes flicker to the lieutenant. I can hear his heart. It sings a song that pings full of question marks, high notes from a xylophone. Madden wonders if she'd let him make that kind of commitment. So he shrugs and says, "I'll think about it. Thank you."

Madden and the lieutenant and I pile into our truck. Ashvi decided to take the bus back with the others, so she waves goodbye and heads to Page Middle. Maybe Madden was right. Maybe she is done with us since their duet (now: trio) is complete.

I'm in the back seat by myself, which means I can pace to-and-fro, window to window, and bark at the cars that dare to whizz past us. Soon, I'm so tired I realize I can't stand another minute, so I collapse in a coil. Madden laughs at me from the front seat.

Silence.

No music, no talking. Just the hum of tires on road. My eyes droop.

The lieutenant shifts in her driver's seat and clears her throat. "So, what piece are you going to play to audition for jazz band?"

And Madden? Madden's emotions explode like smoky shimmery fireworks—*pow kapow pop!* "I could do that?"

The lieutenant ignores the question. "You could play 'Rocket Man.' I love that song."

Madden laughs. "Only if I'm auditioning for a group of octogenarians."

The lieutenant chuckles, and it sounds like the ice on our pond cracking as the sun warms its surface. "It's *jazz band*, Madden. Your target audience isn't exactly spring chickens."

They laugh and giggle their way through song possibilities:

"'Thriller'?"

"Nah, not jazz."

"Some Motown, then."

"Maybe . . ."

"How about a Broadway tune?"

"No way!"

Their banter sounds like a duet, like two very different

instruments playing off each other. It's the first time I've heard them talk this long without it being about diabetes.

"Oh! How about some Trombone Shorty?"

Madden's face quirks. "You think I could play that?"

"Absolutely. We'll get you lessons if you need."

Doubt smells slick and bumpy like raw chicken. "Could we do that?"

The lieutenant shrugs. "What, you think the army doesn't have a few musicians who could give us a lesson or two? Just watch me pull rank here."

They laugh at that, then sit in silence for a while before the lieutenant grins. "'Thriller.' Son, it's a good thing I filed for that transfer to come home. My kid woulda walked up into a jazz band audition with 'Thriller' . . ."

Madden's heart takes a sudden uptick, an adagio. I learned that label in band. "Wait, *you* put in a transfer to come home?"

The lieutenant blinks, and she smells suddenly salty like taffy or tears. "Of course, Madden. I was heartbroken to be overseas when we found out you are a . . ." She stops here, takes a deep breath. She was about to label him a *diabetic*, but she knows that's not what Madden *is*, it's what he *has*. ". . . when we found

268

out you have diabetes. Thank goodness your grand-parents took care of everything until I could get back. I love many things about the military, but they aren't known for their rapidity in situations like that."

I can hear Madden's heart piecing together these surprising new notes. "But you loved that job."

The lieutenant arches her back, looks over her shoulder at the traffic on the highway. "Yeah, well. I love you more."

If I'm understanding all this correctly, the lieutenant *requested* her reassignment? Isn't that like choosing failure? But then she ended up here, home, with Mad-den. That's not failure. It reminds me of those balloons when we learned about chaos theory. They bumped and spun and drifted sideways on the wind, but still they went UP. They didn't *fail*; they adjusted. They found a new path.

The tires hum. Our three heartbeats blend, making an arpeggio. "Mom?" Madden asks.

"Hmmm?"

"What you said earlier. About Dad? That you didn't protect him?"

The lieutenant gulps, nods.

"That wasn't your job, Mom. I'm really sorry dia-betes stole him from us." I can hear Madden swallow past the sudden lump in his throat. "And I want you

to know, well . . . you do a good job of it. Of protecting me."

The lieutenant blinks, and a tear slips down her
face. Madden and I have this in common: we love our
dads. And our path UP looks different from theirs.

"And Mom?"

"Yes?"

"Can I bring a friend with me to that JDRF walk?"

★ 41 ★

BRING IT, DOG

Who wants to go for a walk?"

I leap to my feet and bark, because I am shameless and I have no self-control when it comes to seeing my blue play leash. Madden squats, clips it on.

My ears rotate, perk toward the kitchen. The lieutenant is talking to herself, pacing. She does this sometimes, while she holds her blue screen to her ear. I'll never fully understand humans.

And I think that's okay. I understand what I need to.

"You should've seen him, PopPop," the lieutenant says into her blue screen. "He nailed it. Looked just like you with your saxophone. And they won!"

Madden doesn't seem to hear any of this, based on

his steady, skippy heartbeat. His scent stays drifty calm and sweet, like honeysuckle.

The lieutenant continues. "Yeah, they won state! Right? I'll send you the video, just like last time. Thank you again for that donation. They wouldn't have been able to go to this competition without that.

"And listen. I know you two said that Madden and I needed some space to get to know each other again, but I feel like we're doing great. How about you plan a trip to come see us this summer?"

Madden's silly small ears hear none of this. He leads me outside.

When we get to the park, Madden unclips my vest, my leash. "Go, Zeus!"

The day is warm, and the ice on the pond has almost melted off. Dragonflies buzz about, sewing the air like tiny electric needles. They taste like papercuts, dragonflies, but they're fun to chase. They remind me of Ashvi's flute. I miss Ashvi.

The ground is squishy and cool between my paw pads. So I dig in my back haunches and *BARK BARK BARK BARK BARK!*

I'm halfway around the pond before the ducks realize I'm coming.

YOU! YOU! NO! GO! AWAY! BIG! TEETH!

Big teeth?

I skid to a stop.

They know I'd never actually . . . *do* anything, don't they? They know this is a game?

One brave duck waddles forward while the others paddle out into deep water. He raises his wings like a dare.

YOU WANT SUMMA DIS? BRING IT, DOG!

He's so brave, this one duck, out here talking smack. I feel half my face lift. I'm the Jake here. This duck is the Madden. I may not fully understand humans, but I understand this.

BACK OFF, DOG! I TASTE TERRIBLE AND YOU WILL LIVE WITH REGRET IN YOUR SOUL FOR THE REMAINDER OF YOUR DAYS.

We're cool, duck. We're cool, I say.

The duck's face shifts, if that's possible for a bird. *Duck? Duck?! GOOSE!* He quacks a laugh, and his duck buddies quack along with him, all flustering and flappy. *Ha! And they call US birdbrains!* He begins pacing, flapping his wings in wide, swinging gestures. *Buddy, we're not ducks, we're geese! Branta canadensis, in fact. Canada geese.*

Geese? I squeak. I couldn't be more shocked if I'd hiked my leg on an electric fence. They are geese? I've been labeling these birds as ducks for months, and now I find out they are geese.

Labels can be . . . *wrong*?

My haunches twitch. I scratch at my neck with my paw. I shakeshakeshake and feel tilty because LABELS CAN BE WRONG. *Huh. A flock of geese*, I say.

The birds get all flappy and full of honks again. *A GAGGLE of geese*, the head bird says. *A group of geese is called a gaggle. You really don't know much about birds, do you?*

I . . . know you can fly.

We can do many things, canine. The goose crosses his wings over his broad, feathery chest, taps his flappy foot. *Certainly more than any old scraggly gang of ducks.* The geese all honk out gales of laughter at that.

You're not ducks, I say. *Well, I'll be a puppy's uncle. I thought you were ducks.*

The main goose raises his wings, feathers spread wide. He flaps them at me. Pushy bird.

GEESE! WE. ARE. GEESE. YOU. MANGY. MUTT.

And then he nips me on my leg—BITES ME WITH HIS FLAT, WEIRD, WAXY BILL. *We migrate home tomorrow. Bye, Dog. IF YOU ARE A DOG, THAT IS.* He waddles away, chuckling and snorting. The geese honk a bunch of nonsense at each other, and I proceed to have an identity crisis in which I wonder: *Am* I a dog?! How do I know for sure?

Behind all the terrible goose noise, I hear Madden and his sparkling xylophone chuckle. And then I see why: Ashvi waves from the top of the hill.

I cannot wait to talk to her. I am so much older and wiser since the last time I saw her: yesterday, at the band competition.

Madden's heart leaps out of his chest and runs up next to her like a yipping puppy. The rest of Madden tries to play it cool. He waves back. Wise, because if he tried to talk right now, it'd just come out as a squeak.

I knew she liked us, I bark, but Madden ignores me. Ashvi is perfect. She is hope and doubt. Those two big feelings, side by side, again. Maybe hope can't exist without doubt. Doubt is a fence; hope leaps over fences. But there has to be a fence—otherwise, why leap?

The wind carries Ashvi's flutelike voice across the pond. "Madden, I'm sorry. What I said before the competition? About practicing with Jake." Madden waves her off, but he smells like relief, like a breathy sigh that escapes during a warm hug.

I am so filled with joy, I plow my nose, then my jowls and jaw, then my neck and ribs and back hip through the mud. I flop. I squirm. I wave my paws toward the white-cloud sky. The soft goosh coats my fur and cools my sun-warmed skin. I kick my legs and wriggle wriggle wriggle, coating myself in mud . . .

"Zeus, *no*! Aw man!"

★ 42 ★

I KNOW MY NEXT MISSION

S hut the locker, Zeus."

I nudge Madden's locker shut with my head. *Blam!*

"Spin the lock, Zeus."

I paw at the combination dial built into Madden's locker two, three times. It spins.

"Fist bump, Zeus."

I droop my paw forward and Madden gently pounds it with his knuckles.

It is the Monday following our big Page band win, and in Language Arts, Mr. Nance teaches a poem by a woman who wears the tag Elizabeth Barrett Browning. And would you believe it? It is about a DOG!

FINALLY. A dog named Flush, which seems a very odd name for a pet, since it describes toilet functions and whatnot. Anyway, Mr. Nance dances and recites the poem. I hear a part that sings to me:

> But of thee it shall be said,
> This dog watched beside a bed
> Day and night, unweary—

And I don't know, but I think Flush might be me? I've noticed that about poetry. A lot of it seems to be about me. And yeah, I still love labels. Language speaks to our mind. Music speaks to our soul.

But after the poem, Mr. Nance straightens his bow tie. Clears his throat. "We're not going to review any more poetry this year, kids."

We all groan, me included. No more poetry? No more bubbles or flashlights or crafts or dancing to words?

"I know, but . . ." He pauses. His scent changes to regret. Regret smells like chicken bones—too soft to chew on, too hard to digest. "We have to start prepping for our standardized tests."

More groans. This, I don't understand. *Standardized tests?* All I know is: all forms of the word *test* stink like poo.

The rest of the hour is spent hunched quietly over robot sheets of paper, each student *scratch-scratch-scratch*ing with their pencil points, blackening tiny dots.

After class, Jake falls in step with Madden. Jake's scent is apologetic, like the too-sweet smell of fake sugar put into some of Madden's candy. Madden darkens as if he stepped into a shadow.

"Man, I hate standardized tests," Jake mutters to Madden.

Madden's clouds shift. "Me too. I never do good on those. They make me feel so stupid."

"Yeah," Jake says. His eyes dart quickly to Madden's, then he drifts away. "See you."

Wait.

Not only are these *standardized tests* something that Jake and Madden actually *agree on*, but they make Madden feel stupid? They make him feel LESS THAN OUTSTANDING?

That's it. I know my next mission:

STANDARDIZED TESTS MUST BE DESTROYED.

THE EPI~~LOG~~ DOG

We wait in the visitor room of the prison, but it smells different. Well, the *scents* are all the same: The chicken fried steak in the cafeteria. The human sweat in the gym. The zingy nerves of the people who haven't visited loved ones in a long time.

But the smells *feel* different. These are the smells of my past. My past is like my tail; it is behind me. And like my tail, my past gives me balance, it helps me move and maneuver about the world. But when I try to get a good look at it, it curls *just* out of view. And as a wise dog once said: Tails don't listen. Tails don't have ears. You can't change a tail.

(Me. It was me. I'm the wise dog who said that.)

My future is my nose. It leads me where I need to go. I know I can always trust following it. It is sure and reliable.

Reassignment isn't always terrible. I learned that from the lieutenant. We are all just a bunch of wild balloons, finding our paths UP. I don't want to be reassigned, of course, but if I am? I'll adjust. Find my new, chaotic path.

But I *reallyreallyreally* hope I'm not reassigned. *Don't whimper, Z*, I tell myself.

I whimper.

Dave arrives, and I spinspinspin and *BARK!* I lick him, and he tastes *authentic*. He and Madden fist-bump, chat—*blahblahblah*—and then Madden lays a hand on the knot on top of my head and says:

"I still don't understand how Zeus thinks, but I love him anyway."

Dave grins. "So is Zeus a good fit, then?"

THIS IS IT. MY WHOLE DESTINY FOLLOWS. EVERYTHING I'VE BEEN TRAINING FOR FOR YEARS, EVERYTHING I LOVE AND HOLD DEAR, MY ENTIRE EXISTE—

"Yeah."

Dave smiles. "I thought so."

I blink. I didn't even have time to spiral into a tornado of anxiety there, but if I heard that *yeah* right, then HOORAY, I WILL NOT BE REASSIGNED! And even better, Madden LOVES ME. Which means he's not just keeping me around to make the lieutenant happy. He's keeping me for ME. We are in each other's *orbits* like the spheres in Madden's room. *Orbit* is a fancy human word for *close by*.

I am not a failure. Dave and Madden agree: I am a good fit. I wish this moment could be a fermata moment. That's a label I learned in band. It's a squiggly symbol that means *hold this note*. I want to hold this tasty chicken nugget of a moment forever in my heart.

I love you, Madden! I say with my eyes. Then Dave reaches down and hugs my neck. He is heavy, heavier than I remember. He whispers into my tall, pointy ear, "'Miracles are the natural way of the Universe—our only job is to move our doubting minds out of the way.' Jonathan Lockwood Huie said that."

I don't know what that means, exactly, but I lick him. He tastes salty. And then Madden picks up my leash. And I panic a bit, because what if Madden forgot I love him while Dave was hugging me? So I tell him again, because it's been several seconds: *I love you, Madden.*

Madden smiles, tugs my leash. We leave.

It is the last time I'll ever see Dave. I know this. He can't leave this kennel to visit me. But I also know: he wants me to follow my nose rather than chase my tail.

AUTHOR'S NOTE

Not all heroes wear capes, but many of them wear service dog vests. Service dogs can do amazing things: They can detect an impending seizure in persons with epilepsy. They can calm anxiety and panic attacks in persons with post-traumatic stress disorder (PTSD, as in my previous book about service dogs, *A Dog Like Daisy*). And yes, they can detect blood sugar highs and lows in persons who have diabetes.

No one knows exactly *how* dogs can do this, although many suspect it's due to a dog's keen sense of smell. In doing my research, I heard it said that humans might be able to smell a teaspoonful of sugar in a cup of tea. Dogs can smell that same teaspoon of sugar in an entire pond.

German shepherds like Zeus make good service dogs because they're smart—smart and confident enough to know when to be disobedient and seek out any way possible to help their human. My gratitude to

Brenda Dew and Lesley Adams of Retrieving Independence in Brentwood, Tennessee, for enduring hours of my questions on how this works. Brenda and Lesley pair puppies with prisoners, and the training begins.

According to Brenda and Lesley, incarcerated persons are chosen based on a strict application and interview process. Once it's been determined that they'd make a good service dog trainer, they're trained (yes, the people must be trained, too!) and matched with a puppy when one becomes available. The puppies are about four months old when they enter these programs. This situation is ideal: dogs must be with their humans 24/7 in order to make their training most effective, and incarcerated persons are able to provide that stability for the dogs. They are paid for this work, and they learn skills that benefit them once they reenter society. Also, Brenda notes, the dogs offer a calming influence on all inside the institution, so both dogs and humans benefit from this relationship.

The instruction begins with behavior training (commands like *sit* and *stay*), then moves into scent training. Retrieving Independence has a network of volunteers who have diabetes to aid in the scent training of these dogs. These persons wear flat cotton pads inside their socks, and when their blood sugar spikes or bottoms out, they save that cotton pad in a Ziploc bag in a freezer and label it with the exact blood sugar number. The dogs use these cotton pads to learn the differences between blood sugar highs, lows, and the normal range. Between 80 and 120 milligrams of glucose (sugar) per deciliter is considered a typical normal range. The dogs *then* must be taught that they are smelling the scent on the cotton pad, and not the cotton itself. The process from puppy-in-training to a dog in a vest takes about fourteen months. Through Retrieving Independence, a service dog costs about $15,000 (which is one of the best prices I've heard of for such a highly trained dog!).

Not all dogs are trained this same way, of course. Rebecca Garrett of Borderland, also in Tennessee, teaches regular pet owners how to train their family pets to become diabetic alert dogs. Not every pet has the temperament to do this, of course, but according to Rebecca, if the dog is interested and able, training your pet to alert blood sugar highs and lows can be a very cost-effective tool for your family. More information on both Borderland and Retrieving Independence can be found in the Acknowledgments.

Diabetes is a chronic condition in which the pancreas produces little or no insulin. Insulin is needed to allow sugar (often called glucose) to enter cells to produce energy. Type 1 diabetes (sometimes called juvenile diabetes) is often diagnosed in childhood and requires the medicine and technology you read about in this story; Madden has type 1 diabetes. With type 1 diabetes, the pancreas produces no insulin. It can cause dangerous medical conditions like seizures or comas if medical insulin is not properly balanced and maintained. Type 2 diabetes is far more common in the United States; with type 2, the pancreas produces some insulin and can often be controlled with weight management, diet, and exercise.

As of this writing, the technology for managing type 1 diabetes is as current and realistic as I could make it for a middle schooler like Madden. A continuous glucose monitor (CGM) is attached to the skin and monitors glucose levels. However, because a CGM monitors body fluids slightly differently than other methods, there can be a lag time of five to twenty minutes for the glucose readings to be accurate, and blood sugar can do wild things in that small window of time. Persons wearing a CGM must therefore calibrate this system by backing it up with a traditional fingerprick method two or three times daily. The fingerprick method is much more accurate on a moment-to-moment basis, but it only monitors glucose when the person proactively pricks his/her finger and tests the blood droplet. A CGM monitors glucose patterns and trends over time; the fingerprick method is accurate at that moment. For that reason, many persons with type 1 diabetes use both.

In many cases, however, a diabetic alert dog can be the best solution of all. Dogs trained in this kind of scent detection have very little "lag" time as described by the CGM monitor. They can almost immediately detect abrupt changes in glucose levels. Diabetic alert dogs can be ideal for persons who are very active or who are frequently exposed to hot and cold weather, like people who work outdoors. An excellent book about diabetic alert dogs is *Elle & Coach: Diabetes, the Fight for My Daughter's Life, and the Dog Who Changed Everything* by Stefany Shaheen and Mark Dagostino. In this nonfiction book, we follow Elle's journey from being diagnosed with type 1 diabetes through to adopting Coach, her diabetic alert dog. You will, like I was, be amazed and impressed at the things Coach and dogs like him can do.

And speaking of good literature, below is a list of the poetry Zeus and Madden learn together in their class, the Glorious Study of Labels:

"The Red Wheelbarrow" by William Carlos Williams. Originally published in 1923.

"She sights a Bird—she chuckles" by Emily

Dickinson. Originally published about 1862.

"The Pig" by Roald Dahl. Originally published in 1960.

"Ducks" by F. W. Harvey. Originally published in 1919.

"To Flush, My Dog" by Elizabeth Barrett Browning. Originally published in 1921.

Also, really astute readers know that Zeus isn't actually known as the god of chaos. Smiles to you if you know which god(dess) was known as such!

Finally, more information on foundations that seek a cure for diabetes and foundations that train diabetic alert dogs—and how you can help!—is provided in the Acknowledgments. Because while diabetic alert dogs are heroes, they, like all animals on this planet, count on us humans to take care of them. Let's help these heroes as much as they help us.

ACKNOWLEDGMENTS

"Books are a team sport." My critique group and I are fond of saying that, and it's true. Books are created by teams of story lovers. I'm so grateful for the following teams that helped bring *Zeus, Dog of Chaos* to life:

Thank you to the Writers & Hikers (round two in Damascus!): Sarah Brown, Alisha Klapheke, Erica Rodgers, Court Stevens, and Lauren Thoman. When I started writing *Zeus* on this retreat, it was missing *something*. The drive between Nashville and Damascus, Virginia, with these music lovers gave me the missing piece of the puzzle: middle school band! Plus I love these ladies with my whole heart, and I am so grateful for their friendship.

Thank you, always, to the Society of Children's Book Writers and Illustrators, particularly the Midsouth chapter. SCBWI is the best group of cheerleaders a creator can hope for!

Thank you to Josh Adams of Adams Literary,

whose initial reaction to Zeus was "Awwww!" I'm so grateful to have worked with Josh and Tracey for over a decade. Here's to many more, friends!

Thank you to Ben Rosenthal, my editor, who saw Zeus for the chaotic, loving pup that he is. He made Zeus funnier, made Zeus's relationships more meaningful. I'm grateful for Ben, editorial assistant Tanu Srivastava, copy editor Janet Robbins Rosenberg, production editor Kathryn Silsand, and all at Katherine Tegen Books. Thank you for the beautiful stories you create for young readers!

Thank you to the Juvenile Diabetes Research Foundation (JDRF). Type 1 diabetes is sometimes called "juvenile" diabetes, because it's often diagnosed in childhood. This organization does lifesaving research for those living with diabetes. Diabetes is an "invisible" illness, meaning those who live with it often don't look sick. It can be a challenge to get others to understand how serious diabetes truly can be, because when it's managed well, the person can do anything he or she wants. Check out www.jdrf.org for more information, including how to find a walkathon near you! A portion of the sales of *Zeus, Dog of Chaos* will go to the JDRF.

Thank you to friend Mike Edwards, who answered numerous questions about living with and managing diabetes (and particularly how that applied to middle school band!). He is a mentor to others who have been recently diagnosed, and he was patient with my barrage of questions. One thing Mike would tell you is that a student like Madden would probably have a closer relationship with the school nurse than what I've portrayed here. Anything else incorrect in this story is my misunderstanding. Mike pointed me toward "Diabetic Danica," a YouTube channel dedicated to providing people with diabetes more information about the latest products, medicines, and technology. Thank you to Danica, a registered nurse and person with diabetes, for sharing her knowledge far and wide!

Thank you to Brenda Dew and Lesley Adams of Retrieving Independence. Brenda and Lesley are two dynamos who work with incarcerated people to train dogs as diabetic alert animals. Many service dogs are trained by people in prison, inside prison walls. It is a system that benefits everyone involved, and I'm grateful for programs like Retrieving Independence. They taught me so much about how diabetic alert dogs are trained. You can learn more about the program (and donate to them!) at retrievingindependence.org. A portion of all sales of *Zeus, Dog of Chaos* will go toward Retrieving Independence.

Thank you to Rebecca Garrett of Borderland. Rebecca began training dogs to assist people with diabetes when her own daughter was diagnosed with type 1 diabetes at age ten. Rebecca trained their family pet to assist her daughter, and Borderland was born! Borderland allows families to train their own pets to become diabetic alert dogs. It's a fascinating program.

Thank you to the *real* Page Middle School Band! Particularly its fearless leader, band director Carol Strayer, and its wonderful instructor Evan Burton. Ms. Strayer and Mr. Burton let me sit in on dozens of their classroom sessions in the spring of 2018. Their rapport with the students is second to none, and the students give their all in return. Support your school's music and arts programs!

Thank you to Julie Caudle, Page Middle School's librarian, who helped make the connections needed for this story. Schools need great libraries and librarians, and "my" Page Middle School has exactly that! #librariansaremyrockstars

Thank you to all the booksellers, librarians, teachers, bloggers, festival organizers, parents, and grandparents who share books with kids! There is no better way to grow empathy than through a story. I am so very grateful for all you do to help readers find stories they love. Keep sharing stories and growing empathy worldwide—you make a difference word by word, page by page.

Thank you to Byron, Chloe, and Jack, always. I am grateful for the chaos in our lives, every single day. I love you!

TURN THE PAGE FOR A SNEAK PEEK AT
LUNA HOWLS AT THE MOON!

★ 1 ★

NOT ALMOST

Most of my clients don't mind when I lick their tears away. Others want me to roll over and show them my belly. Still others just want the big, soft, blinky eyes coupled with a slow wag. Or a goofy jangle of my tags. Or letting my tongue loll out. Sometimes I chase my tail, even though it makes me dizzy and I know I'm never going to catch that rascal. But I do it because it makes the client happy. It's all about the client. Reading them and responding. Making them feel safe. Secure. Confident. Each of us has a different hole that needs filling. My job as a therapy dog is to find the shape of that hole and fill it. That's why my name is Luna. Just like the moon, I change shape. I become what others need to see.

It works like . . . a yawn. *Yaaaawwwwwn.* When someone yawns, others yawn. It's catching, but in a subtle, gentle way. That's how it feels to pick up on others' emotions.

A yawn? My classmate Goliath scoffs when I ask him if that's how the job works for him too. *Hey, fellas! Luna here says her job is a big yawn. Maybe you need a new line of work, kid. Something more exciting—a rodeo dog, maybe? The circus?*

All the other dogs huddled in this too-bright church basement wag their tails, rattle their tags, sneeze. They laugh, but the emotion around their chuckles isn't joy. It feels sharper, darker; honed to pierce like a thorn.

My instinct is to be upset, but duty says I should remain calm. I often have to defy my instincts because my training says that I should be both calm and calming. Duty over instinct, always. So I laugh too, because I don't want the others at Therapy Dogs Worldwide to think I'm weird or different or something.

The only dog who doesn't laugh is Samwise. Samwise has her 400-visit pin. That makes her a Distinguished Therapy Dog by TDW standards, and that's all you need to know about Samwise. Impressive.

Seriously, though, Luna. Take it from me. Goliath

twitches and scratches his perky chihuahua ear. He's the itchiest dog I've ever met. *You get too close*, Goliath says. *You FEEL too much. All your clients want? To give you a pat here, a hug there. That's it. You don't owe them anything more than that. You need to grow thicker fur, kid.*

I hate it when Goliath calls me kid, because we're the same age. That, and I'm about four times his size. I'm a silver Labrador, but Goliath makes me feel like a rusty mutt. We went through class together at Therapy Dogs Worldwide. Just because he earned his 50-visit pin faster than any other dog in our class—faster than any other dog in TDW history—he thinks his breath doesn't stink. His head's gotten so big I don't know how they get his leash on.

The light in this stuffy room shifts, and I feel sudden smiles in the air. "Okay, everyone," says Barb, the leader of the local TDW chapter. I love her, so I let her know with a tail wag. "The photographer here wants to get several shots for the *American-Statesman*. All of Austin will read about what good dogs you are!"

Good dogs. We wag. The joy caused by eight dogs all wagging tails together feels like a perfect slant of sunshine.

"Okay, so, Roy," Barb says, turning to the photographer. "We're here tonight celebrating the dogs who just got their fifty-visit pin. Once the dogs have made fifty different visits to clients, they become official TDW therapy dogs, and we reward their hard work with one of these." Barb holds up a small blue pin, and rays of light ping off it. It shines like a tiny star. It's more beautiful than greasy sausage.

"That'll be yours soon, Luna," Tessa whispers to me. Tessa. She's my human. Well, I have lots of humans in my line of work, but she's the main one. Tessa makes me imagine a honeybee: hardworking, always thinking of her hive. She rubs my soft ear and it feels so good my back leg thumps *thank you thank you thank you*.

"So let's start with a photo of all the dogs who have their fifty-visit pin, then," the photographer, Roy, says. He waves his camera at a colorful sign. "Stand around that banner."

Every dog in the room moves toward the sign. Every dog but me. The air in this creepy-drippy basement darkens, and I feel like that perfect slant of sun has disappeared behind a cloud. I sulk.

"Cheese!" the humans all shout, and I drool like I do every time humans take photos, because why do they always shout that?! Roy's camera pops like firecrackers. He shifts his camera sideways and takes more photos. He changes positions and takes more photos. He stands on a chair and takes more photos.

Alone I sit. I sulk harder. The air gets heavier. *Grow thicker fur*, Goliath said. How would that help? Every strand of my fur feels like a tiny rag, soaking up all the moods around me. How would having *more* fur help? What's wrong with me that I *feel* so much? All the time?

"So why aren't they wearing vests?" Roy asks, waving the lens of his camera over the gang of dogs between clicks. "They're service dogs, right?"

Barb smiles. "I'm glad you asked that, Roy. No, they aren't service dogs. They're therapy dogs. A bit like emotional support dogs, but they comfort many people, not just one. Some of these dogs visit hospitals, some visit retirement centers. Some are placed in schools and libraries to help with reading programs. Some work with therapists and counselors as they meet with their clients. But therapy dogs wear bandannas instead of vests because they are meant to be hugged and petted as often as possible. These dogs are *heroes*."

That's what I want to be too. A *hero*. And I'm almost there. When I get that pin, everyone will know it. They will know I put duty first. I think of that shiny pin and I can't help but wag. And so, the air shifts again. Shimmery this time, like starlight poking holes in the dark. I smile and my tongue lolls out of my mouth. I will be a star.

Barb looks over at Tessa and me, standing on the opposite side of the room, alone. Her face changes, and I feel her *pity*. *Pity* feels green and tight and sour like wild apples.

"Oh, can we get one more photo with Luna in it?" Barb asks. "She's only nine visits away from her fifty-visit pin. Such a good girl."

I love Barb. I tell her this again with my tail. I stand, ready to be photographed and famous.

"Can't," Roy says, slamming his camera equipment into multiple bags and zipping them shut. "Gotta go shoot the school board meeting next."

Goliath snickers loudly, and the others follow suit. *So close there, Luna. SO CLOSE. You sure seem to live a life of almosts.*

What a bunch of thorns.

As if she hears them, my honeybee Tessa scratches my neck. "Nine visits, girl. Almost there. The next party will be for you."

Nine visits. Nine more client visits and I'll get my own tiny star pinned to my bandanna. The tiny star that will let everyone know I'm not weird or different or something. That I take my duty seriously. That I'm not *almost*.

★ 2 ★

UNCERTAINTY IS LIKE
DRINKING MUDDY WATER

Who's ready to go to work?" Tessa asks, and I bark and wag and spinspinspin as a reply. Tessa knots my bandanna around my neck. It's crisp and red and it smells like months of comforting kid humans. Like laughter and tears and hugs and sighs.

I love the routine Tessa and I have. I study feelings. I try to define emotions. I don't understand them all, and sometimes they overwhelm me. That's when I remember my duty: calm and calming. But the routine is nice: wake, eat, work, sleep. Quiet habits fill our days.

Tessa tugs the bandanna around my neck and gives me a delicious scratch. We feel excited and a bit nervous today, it seems; it feels like the thrill of riding in a car with the windows down, all bugs and wind and sun, but the road is curvy and bumpy.

We are trying something *new*.

"This group session will be good," Tessa says, running her fingers over my sleek ears. But it sounds like she's saying this to herself rather than to me. Humans do that a lot to dogs: tell them things they need to hear themselves. Things like *she's a good girl* and *I love you*. Tessa continues, "I've decided we're going to focus on managing emotions in this group. My mentor says group sessions can sometimes get out of hand, but I don't think we need to worry about that with these kids. We know these kids, don't we, Luna? They're great. It'll be great."

This group thing: it's not our regular routine. It's new. New feels *uncertain*, like drinking muddy water. You're never quite sure what you're getting from a mud puddle. But I trust Tessa. And I trust these clients of ours.

It is the orange part of the day, and sun paints everything the color of poppies. Tessa lifts a plastic tub full of art supplies out of the back of her car and settles it on her hip. But instead of us going to our cozy trailer in the church parking lot like we usually do, she uses a key to unlock the door down to the church basement. The same basement where I didn't become famous because they didn't take my picture for the paper. *Almost.*

I don't like this place. I pause going down the narrow wooden steps.

Tessa must sense my hesitation, because she smiles her sunflower smile, the one that turns people toward her. "We have to meet as a group down here, Luna. Not enough room in our trailer. We can be brave."

It's not a question, and I love that about Tessa. She knows when to ask for bravery, and when to announce it's needed.

I totter down the stairs and into the drippy, weird basement. The lights flicker on in sections like lightning. I hear a toilet running, so I seek it out down a dark hallway and take huge gulps of cold water before we start our day. *Whew.* Much better. There's nothing in the world a little toilet water can't fix.

When I return, Tessa has spilled colorful art supplies all over the tabletops, and my tail wags because ART! Art smells like glue and paint and crayons and oils and it makes humans feel hummy happy, like shimmery, buzzing birds sipping sugar water.

Anticipation is like hearing the word *walk*, seeing the leash, but then not leaving right away. It's what I feel now. I wait for my clients to arrive. Should I sit? No, too casual. Stand? Too formal. I pace, because I'm uncertain what to expect with all my clients here in

9

one room, together. Tessa feels the same. She chews on a piece of rubber, blows a bubble, and *pop*! Cracks it against her lips.

Caleb arrives first. My ears perk toward him. "Where's the chessboard?"

Tessa smiles. "I have it, but I thought we might start with some art first."

Caleb feels as hesitant as a dog on a too-short leash. My whiskers twitter. But he enters and picks a seat in front of a rainbow of oil paints. His knee bounces beneath the table and the paints dance across the table-top before he realizes that his long, lanky legs are the ones making them hop.

Without asking Tessa, Caleb leaps up, takes one of the bowls of water that are supposed to be for art, and places it near my paws. He doesn't say anything, doesn't even meet my eyes, but he seems to know I was thirsty earlier. I thank him with my tail. He drops back into his chair and his knees bounce more.

Amelia and Hector arrive at the same moment. My nostrils twitch between the two of them, trying to untangle the air around them so I can sense each one. Amelia hugs me quickly (she smells like grass) and then glides to the paints too. Hector bumps down the stairs with his bike over his shoulder, then chooses a spot far down the table, next to a pile of wrinkly magazines and a snarl of scissors.

Waterfall. Rock. Shadow. That's what these three are.

I feel the Knot approach before she even enters. She bang bang bangs down the basement steps in her tooth-boots and falls into a metal chair that groans in reply. "Sorry I'm late."

Beatrice the Knot sits in front of a huge lump of clay. Her jeans are worn and spattered with paint, almost as if she got a head start on arting.

Tessa talks about groups and growth, and I stand nearby and *sniiiiiiiiiffff*. Twitch my whiskers. Adjust my ears. It's odd, all these feelings together, like trying to sort through the smells wafting off a lovely garbage can.

And then they *create*. Art makes humans see things the same way the artist sees them, and it makes humans see things differently than they have before. Both same and different. And creating art makes human feelings smooth out, brighten, clarify, like a sheen of ice over a nighttime pond.

When the Knot and the Shadow, the Waterfall and the Rock start arting, they focus. They stick tongues out of the corners of their mouths. They sit less erect. They breathe evenly.

It's working! I wag at Tessa. These clients are loosening, lightening.

11

Beatrice moves from massaging a lump of clay to pounding it. She stands to pound better, *pound pound pound*. She doesn't seem to notice the glare that Caleb shoots her as the paints leap around the table. Amelia grins down at her piece of paper and keeps swooshing colors across it like comets. Hector cuts apart panels of a comic strip from a newspaper, *snip snip snip*.

Beatrice pounds more, lifts her chin at Hector's comic. "You know, at my school they won't let us read graphic novels for book reports? Isn't that the stupidest thing you've ever heard?"

Pound pound pound. Snip snip snip. The room is silent.

Caleb bites his bottom lip. We feel *undecided*, I realize. But he says it anyway: "Probably not THE stupidest, but yes. Pretty ridiculous."

Beatrice pauses the pounding. I can't get a read on her feelings because we're swirling through so many so quickly. "You like graphic novels?"

Caleb nods once. "I do."

"Which ones?" The way Beatrice says it, it sounds more like blame than a question.

"*Bone. Amulet.* And I read lots of comics."

"Marvel or DC?"

"Marvel, of course."

Beatrice smirks, and if I were human, I might be

confused by that. But I know by her scent that she's satisfied with that answer. *This is working!* I wag more.

Pound pound pound. Snip snip snip. The room is silent again.

"You could start a petition, you know." Caleb bites his lip again, dabs his paintbrush in gray paint. He is painting a chessboard, I see.

"A what?" *Pound pound pound.*

"A petition. It's a formally written request. A document that—"

"I *know* what a petition *is*!" Beatrice cocks her head at Caleb, and the bun on top of her head slides around like a tennis ball. I copy her; I cock my head too. Always let the client take the lead. Duty first. "I just didn't know what you meant by that."

"You could draw up a petition to change that rule about graphic novels. Write something up on your computer. Get all your friends to sign it. Give it to the administrators. Maybe they'd change that rule." Caleb says all of this without once looking up from the gray-and-white chessboard he's painting.

Beatrice narrows her eyes at him. I narrow my eyes too. Our lips flatten. "You don't know if that would work," she says.

"I do know."

It is quiet, so he continues. "At my school there was

this form we all had to fill out. And on it, you had to pick your race. White, African American, Native American, Asian American . . . you know. But checking *white* felt like I was choosing my dad's family over my mom's and checking *Black* felt like I was choosing Mom's family over Dad's. You'd think they'd have a box that said *Multiracial*, but they didn't. I knew they wanted me to check *Other*, you know? But I didn't like that term. *Other.* So I started a petition where we could check more than one box."

It is the most I've ever heard Caleb talk. He dips his paintbrush in gray paint again. It is still quiet, but Beatrice wears a small grin. Amelia nods. Hector stops snipping.

"And I won," Caleb tells his chessboard. "Now I check more than one box."

Beatrice nods. Knocks the table. This story *satisfies* her, like a nice steak taco. "More than one box. Dude. I get that."

They continue to art.

Pound pound pound. Snip snip snip.

Beatrice leans over Amelia's painting. "Wow! Wouldja look at that!"

Amelia burns like she's had too much sun on her skin, but she beams.

"Is that a bomb?" Beatrice says, pointing at Amelia's paper. Amelia nods.

Tessa scoots over there, and I feel her have a flutter of panic at this. "A bomb?" She leans over the painting. Her heart calms and she says, "Oh! It's exploding with flowers! How lovely, Amelia."

"My grammy used to say this thing," Beatrice says quietly. "She always said she wasn't fragile like a flower; she was fragile like a *bomb*."

Beatrice clears her throat and tries to hide the sudden shine that's appeared on her eyes. The word *grammy* always makes Bea choke up. She hooks her thumbs in the loops on her paint-spattered jeans and bounces on her toes. Amelia smiles large, larger, and nods.

Tessa's eyes widen. "Amelia! I'm so glad to see you using your nonverbal language with Beatrice!"

Tessa no sooner finishes horking up those words than she wishes she could lap them back up again, like vomit. Amelia's face lines slant down sharply, and instead of now burning like sun on skin, she burns like a match.